Roverandom

WORKS BY J.R.R. TOLKIEN

The Hobbit
Leaf by Niggle
On Fairy-Stories
Farmer Giles of Ham
The Homecoming of Beorhtnoth
The Lord of the Rings
The Adventures of Tom Bombadil
The Road Goes Ever On (*with Donald Swann*)
Smith of Wootton Major

WORKS PUBLISHED POSTHUMOUSLY

Sir Gawain and the Green Knight, Pearl, and Sir Orfeo
The Father Christmas Letters
The Silmarillion
Pictures by J.R.R. Tolkien
Unfinished Tales
The Letters of J.R.R. Tolkien
Finn and Hengest
Mr Bliss
The Monsters and the Critics & Other Essays
Roverandom

THE HISTORY OF MIDDLE-EARTH BY CHRISTOPHER TOLKIEN

I · The Book of Lost Tales, Part One
II · The Book of Lost Tales, Part Two
III · The Lays of Beleriand
IV · The Shaping of Middle-earth
V · The Lost Road and Other Writings
VI · The Return of the Shadow
VII · The Treason of Isengard
VIII · The War of the Ring
IX · Sauron Defeated
X · Morgoth's Ring
XI · The War of the Jewels
XII · The Peoples of Middle-earth

ALSO BY CHRISTINA SCULL & WAYNE G. HAMMOND

J.R.R. Tolkien: Artist & Illustrator

Roverandom

by

J.R.R. Tolkien

Edited by

CHRISTINA SCULL
WAYNE G. HAMMOND

Houghton Mifflin Company
BOSTON NEW YORK

Library of Congress Cataloging-in-Publication Data

Tolkien, J. R. R. (John Ronald Reuel), 1892-1973.
Roverandom / by J.R.R. Tolkien : edited by Christina Scull,
Wayne G. Hammond.
p. cm.
Summary: A dog who has been turned into a toy dog encounters rival
wizards and experiences various adventures on the moon with
giant spiders, dragon moths, and the Great White Dragon.
ISBN 0-395-89871-4
ISBN 0-395-95799-0 (pbk.)
[1. Dogs—Fiction. 2. Dragons—Fiction. 3. Fantasy.]
I. Scull,Christina. II. Hammond, Wayne G. III. Title.
PZ7.T5744RO 1998
[Fic]—dc21 97-36882 CIP AC

Printed in the United States of America
QUM 10 9 8 7 6 5 4 3 2 1

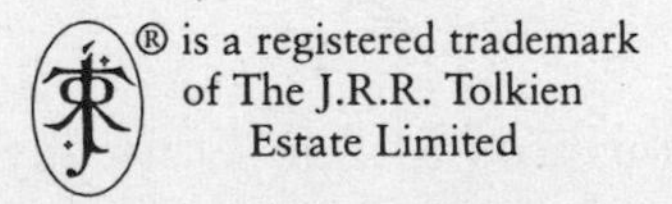

This book is dedicated
to the memory of
Michael Hilary Reuel Tolkien
1920–1984

Contents

Introduction

IN THE SUMMER OF 1925 J.R.R. Tolkien, his wife Edith, and their sons John (nearly eight), Michael (nearly five), and Christopher (not yet one year old) went on holiday to Filey, a town on the Yorkshire coast which is still popular with tourists. It was an unexpected holiday, in celebration of Tolkien's appointment as Rawlinson and Bosworth Professor of Anglo-Saxon at Oxford, which he was to take up on 1 October that year; and it was perhaps intended as a period of rest for him before he not only assumed that post, but for two terms would continue to teach at the University of Leeds, as his old and new appointments overlapped. For three or four weeks at Filey – as explained below, the dates are uncertain – the Tolkiens rented an Edwardian cottage which may have belonged to the local postmaster, built high on a cliff overlooking the beach and the sea. From this vantage point the view to the east was unobstructed, and young John Tolkien was thrilled when for two or three beautiful evenings the full moon rose out of the sea and shone a silver 'path' across the water.

At this time Michael Tolkien was extremely fond of a miniature toy dog, made of lead and painted black and white. He ate with it and slept with it, and carried it around with him; he was reluctant to let it go even to have his hand washed. But during the holiday at Filey he went for a walk with his father and elder brother, and in the excitement of skimming stones into the sea put his toy down, onto the beach of white shingle. Against this background the tiny black and white dog became virtually invisible, and was lost. Michael was heartbroken when his toy could not be found, although the two older boys and their father searched for it that day and the next.

The loss of a favourite toy is of great moment to a child, and no doubt it was with this in mind that Tolkien was inspired to invent an 'explanation' for the occurrence: a story in which a real dog, named Rover, is turned into a toy by a wizard, is lost on a beach by a boy very much like Michael, meets a comical 'sand-sorcerer', and has adventures on the moon and under the sea. At least, that is the full story of *Roverandom*, as it was finally set down on paper. That it did not emerge fully formed, but was devised and told in several parts, might be deduced from its episodic nature, and from its length; and in fact this is verified by a tantalizingly brief entry in Tolkien's diary (written almost certainly in 1926 as part of a résumé of events of 1925) about the composition of *Roverandom* at Filey: 'The tale of "Roverandom" written to amuse John (and myself as it grew) got done.' Unhappily it is not possible to know exactly what Tolkien meant by 'got done' – no more, perhaps, than that the complete story (as it then stood) was told during the holiday. The parenthetical note, however, confirms that the tale did indeed grow in the telling.

It is curious that only John is mentioned in this diary statement, when it was Michael's misfortune which lay behind the story of Rover. It may be that Michael was satisfied with its earliest episode, which explained the disappearance of his toy, and was less interested than John in its continuation. Tolkien himself clearly warmed to the tale, which becomes more sophisticated as it proceeds. But it is nowhere recorded, and no one can now say, exactly in what form *Roverandom* was originally conceived – whether all of its clever twists of language and its allusions to myths and legends, for example, were part of the story from the beginning, or were added when *Roverandom* was at last written down.

Tolkien also wrote in his diary, after the same interval of a few months, that the family went to Filey (from Leeds) on 6 September 1925 and remained there until 27 September. But at least the first of these dates cannot be correct (and indeed is mistakenly recorded in the diary as a Saturday rather than a Sunday). Given that John Tolkien's memory of the full moon shining upon the sea is still vivid, and that the sight was surely the inspiration for Rover's journey along a 'moon-path' early in *Roverandom*, the Tolkiens must have been at Filey during the period of the full moon, which in September 1925 began on Tuesday the 2nd. They can also be placed at Filey, more definitely, in the afternoon of Saturday, 5 September, when the north-east coast of England was struck by a terrific storm. Again John Tolkien's memory is vivid, and it is supported by newspaper reports. The sea rose hours before the scheduled high tide, swept over the sea wall and across the promenade at Filey, devastated structures along the shore, and threw the beach into upheaval – destroying in the process any remaining hope of finding Michael's toy. Fierce winds shook the Tolkiens' cottage so much that they were kept awake into the night, fearing that the roof would come off. John Tolkien remembers his father telling the two older boys a story to keep them calm, and that it was at this time that he began to tell them about the dog Rover who became the enchanted toy 'Roverandom'. The storm itself no doubt inspired the late episode in *Roverandom* in which the ancient Sea-serpent begins to awaken, and in so doing causes a great disturbance in the weather. ('When he undid a curl or two in his sleep, the water heaved and shook and bent people's houses and spoilt their repose for miles and miles around' [p. 76].)

There is no evidence that *Roverandom* was written down while Tolkien was at Filey. However, one of the five illustrations he made for the story, the lunar landscape reproduced in this book, is dated 1925, and it is conceivable that it was drawn at Filey during that summer. Three of the remaining illustrations for *Roverandom* date specifically from September 1927, while the Tolkiens were on holiday at Lyme Regis on the south coast of England: *The White Dragon Pursues Roverandom & the Moondog*, inscribed to John Tolkien; *House Where 'Rover' Began His Adventures as a 'Toy'*, inscribed to Christopher Tolkien; and the splendid watercolour *The Gardens of the Merking's Palace*. On each of these is written the month and year; another drawing, of Rover arriving on the moon riding upon the seagull, Mew, is inscribed '1927–8'. All of these pictures are also reproduced in the present book. The evidence of the September 1927 illustrations suggests that *Roverandom* was retold at Lyme Regis, perhaps because the Tolkiens were once again on holiday by the sea and recalled the events at Filey only two years earlier. The inscription to Christopher Tolkien on *House Where 'Rover' Began His Adventures as a 'Toy'* suggests as well that Christopher was now old enough to appreciate *Roverandom* (he was of course only an infant in September 1925), and that the story may have been retold at least partly because he had not heard it on the previous occasion.

This apparent revival of interest in *Roverandom* in summer 1927 may have been the spur that led Tolkien at last to commit the story to paper; for he seems to have done so later that year, probably during the Christmas holidays. So we are inclined to think – and we can only conjecture, in the absence of dated manuscripts or other firm evidence – on the basis of two interesting (if admittedly tenuous) points. Each of these concerns the end of chapter 2 of *Roverandom*, where it is told how the Great White Dragon is disturbed by Roverandom and his friend the moon-dog and pursues them in a wild chase. The dragon is described as often a troublemaker: 'Sometimes he let real red and green flames out of his cave when he was having a dragon-feast or was in a tantrum; and clouds of smoke were frequent. Once or twice he had been known to turn the whole moon red, or put it out altogether. On such uncomfortable occasions the Man-in-the-Moon . . . went down into the cellars, uncorked his best spells, and got things cleared up as quick as possible' (pp. 33–4). In the present episode his pursuit of the two dogs is stopped by the Man-in-the-Moon only in the nick of time, by a magic spell shot at the dragon's stomach. Because of this 'the next eclipse was a failure, for the dragon was too busy licking his tummy to attend to it' (p. 36) – a reference to the notion, established in the earlier passage, that lunar eclipses are caused by dragon-smoke.

Elements of this chapter of *Roverandom* – one of which (a troublesome dragon on the moon) certainly was part of the story in September 1927, as shown by the dated illustration – also appear, in a strikingly similar form, in an unpublished portion of the story-letter Tolkien wrote to his children in December of that year in the guise of 'Father Christmas'. In this, one of the remarkable series of 'Father Christmas' letters Tolkien wrote between 1920 and 1943, the Man-in-the-Moon visits the North Pole and drinks rather too much brandy while eating plum pudding and playing 'snapdragon'. He falls asleep and is pushed under the sofa by the North Polar Bear, where he remains until the next day. In his absence dragons come out on the moon and make such a great smother that they cause an eclipse. The Man-in-the-Moon is forced to hurry back and work a terrific magic to set things right.

The similarities between this fiction and the Great White Dragon episode in *Roverandom* are too great to be coincidental; and from these one can reasonably suppose that Tolkien had *Roverandom* in his thoughts while writing his 'Father Christmas' letter in December 1927. Whether he introduced the notion of moon-dragons causing eclipses first in the letter, or drew for that purpose upon a conception already existing in *Roverandom*, it is impossible to say; but the two works must be related.

The Christmas holidays offered Tolkien time away from his academic responsibilities, in which *Roverandom* could have been written down; and although it is not definite that he did so in December 1927, one other clue points to that date, at least as a *terminus a quo* for the earliest (undated) extant text: the reference in *Roverandom* to a failed eclipse. In the earliest text 'the next eclipse was a failure' (as quoted above) is followed by the note 'the astronomers [> photographers] said so'. And this indeed was the prevailing opinion, reported in the *Times* of London, of the total lunar eclipse that occurred on 8 December 1927 but was hidden from observers in England by clouds. On this point the 1927 'Father Christmas' letter is once again useful, for it dates the eclipse that occurred in the Man-in-the-Moon's absence precisely to 8 December, and thereby confirms Tolkien's knowledge of the real-world event.

The earliest extant text of *Roverandom* is one of four versions among the Tolkien papers in the Bodleian Library, Oxford. Unhappily one-fifth of it has been lost, equivalent to the present chapter 1 and the first half of chapter 2. The remainder survives on twenty-two pages, written quickly in an occasionally difficult hand on a variety of blank sheets (torn possibly from school exercise books), and with numerous emendations. This text was followed by three typewritten versions, likewise undated, in the course of which Tolkien progressively enlarged the story and made many improvements of expression and detail but no major change of plot. The first typescript, on thirty-nine heavily corrected pages, was closely based on the manuscript and has been of great help in deciphering the less legible parts of the earlier version. But the typescript is notably distinguished from its predecessor towards the end, where the passage in which Rover is restored to his original shape and size (before almost an anticlimax, now a dramatic as well as humorous moment) was greatly expanded. The new text was entitled originally *The Adventures of Rover*, but Tolkien altered the heading in pen to *Roverandom*, thereafter the title he preferred.

The second of the three typescripts breaks off, apparently by conscious decision of the author, after only nine pages, with only a few lines on the final sheet. It extends from the beginning of the story to the point where the moon 'began to lay its shining path on the water' (cf. below, chapter 2, p. 19). In addition, a fragment of writing is typed on what is now the verso of one sheet, which was immediately rejected by Tolkien and the text taken up again, further revised, and continued on the recto. As far as it goes, the second typescript incorporates revisions noted on the first and includes some further improvements. But it is perhaps more important to note the neat appearance of this version, compared with the first typescript. Tolkien now was concerned with matters of presentation, such as typing page numbers on the sheets rather than adding them later in pen, and breaking dialogue into paragraphs to indicate different speakers, whereas before (in what is clearly a working document) it was sometimes run on. Also the new typescript includes only a handful of manuscript emendations, all carefully made and for most part only of typographical errors.

This improved manner of presentation leads us to suspect that Tolkien prepared the second typescript for submission to his publisher, George Allen & Unwin, towards the end of 1936. At that time *The Hobbit* had been accepted with enthusiasm, and although it was only in production and had not yet proved a success, on the strength of it Tolkien was invited to submit other children's stories to be considered for publication. He obliged by sending to Allen & Unwin his picture book *Mr. Bliss*, his mock-medieval story *Farmer Giles of Ham*, and *Roverandom*. If, as we think, the fragmentary second typescript of *Roverandom* was made for this purpose, it may be that Tolkien abandoned it because its text still was not wholly to his liking – or perhaps because, like the preceding drafts, it was made on sheets torn apparently from exercise books, with one long edge slightly ragged, and the author wished his work to have a more professional appearance.

Indeed the third and latest typescript of *Roverandom* is neatly typed (although not without emendations) complete on sixty sheets of commercial bond paper (although not entirely uniform); and it was here that chapter divisions were introduced, together with further changes, small but numerous, of dialogue and description, and of punctuation and the division of paragraphs. This is almost certainly the text that Tolkien submitted to Allen & Unwin and that the chairman of the firm, Stanley Unwin, gave to his young son Rayner to appraise.

In a report dated 7 January 1937 Rayner Unwin found the story 'well written and amusing'; but despite his positive review it was not accepted for publication. *Roverandom* was apparently one of the 'short fairy stories in various styles' that Tolkien had (it was thought) practically ready for publication in October 1937, as Stanley Unwin noted in a memo; but by then *The Hobbit* was so successful that Allen & Unwin wanted a sequel, with more about hobbits, above all else, and *Roverandom* seems never again to have been considered by either author or publisher. Tolkien's attention now became primarily directed towards the 'new Hobbit', the work that would become his masterpiece: *The Lord of the Rings*.

It is not too much to say that *The Lord of the Rings* might not have come into being were it not for stories like *Roverandom*; for their popularity with the Tolkien children, and with Tolkien himself, led at last to a more ambitious work – *The Hobbit* – and so to its sequel. For the most part, these stories were ephemeral. Few were written down, and of those not many were finished. Tolkien settled happily into his role as a storyteller to his children, from at least 1920 when he wrote the first of the 'Father Christmas' letters. There were also stories of the villain Bill Stickers with his adversary Major Road Ahead, of the very small man Timothy Titus, and of the flamboyant Tom Bombadil, who was based on a Dutch doll that belonged to Michael Tolkien. None of these went very far, although Tom Bombadil later found a niche in poems and in *The*

Lord of the Rings. An extremely odd tale of greater length, *The Orgog*, was written in 1924 and is extant in a typescript; but it is both unfinished and undeveloped.

In contrast *Roverandom* is complete and well-crafted; and it is further distinguished among Tolkien's children's fiction of this period for the unrestrained delight with which its author indulged in wordplay. It contains a richness of near-homonyms (*Persia* and *Pershore*), and of onomatopoeia and alliteration ('yaps and yelps, and yammers and yowls, growling and grizzling, whickering and whining, snickering and snarling, mumping and moaning', p. 20), of descriptive lists humorous by their length (such as the 'paraphernalia, insignia, symbols, memoranda, books of recipes, arcana, apparatus, and bags and bottles of miscellaneous spells' in Artaxerxes' workshop, p. 81), and of unexpected turns of phrase ('[The Man-in-the-Moon] vanished immediately into thin air; and anybody who has never been there will tell you how extremely thin the moon-air is', p. 26). It includes as well a number of 'childish' colloquialisms, such as *whizz*, *splosh*, *tummy*, and *uncomfy*, which are of particular interest for their like is rarely met with in Tolkien's published writings, having been omitted *ab initio* in his manuscripts or deleted in revision (as *tummy* was altered in *The Hobbit* to *stomach*). Here they are surely survivals from the story as it was originally told orally to the Tolkien children.

That Tolkien also included in *Roverandom* words such as *paraphernalia*, and *phosphorescent, primordial*, and *rigmarole*, is refreshing in these later days when such language is considered too 'difficult' for young children – a view with which Tolkien would have disagreed. 'A good vocabulary,' he once wrote (April 1959), 'is not acquired by reading books written according to some notion of the vocabulary of one's age-group. It comes from reading books above one' (*Letters of J.R.R. Tolkien* [1981], pp. 298–9).

Roverandom is remarkable too for the variety of biographical and literary materials that went into its making. First among them of course was Tolkien's own family, and the author himself: in *Roverandom* the Tolkien parents and children are seen or (in baby Christopher's case) referred to, the cottage and beach at Filey appear in three chapters, Tolkien several times expresses his feelings about litter and pollution, and events of the 1925 holiday – the moon shining upon the sea, the great storm, and above all the loss of Michael's toy dog – are elements in the tale. To these Tolkien added a wealth of references to myth and fairy-story, to Norse sagas, and to traditional and contemporary children's literature: to the Red and White Dragons of British legend, to Arthur and Merlin, to mythical sea-dwellers (mermaids, Niord, and the Old Man of the Sea among many), and to the Midgard serpent, alongside borrowings from, or at least echoes of, the 'Psammead' books of E. Nesbit, Lewis Carroll's *Through the Looking-glass* and *Sylvie and Bruno*, even Gilbert and Sullivan. It is a wide range, but these diverse materials combined well in Tolkien's hands, with little incongruity and much amusement – for those who recognize the allusions.

We identify and discuss many of Tolkien's sources (definite or probable) for *Roverandom* – as also obscure words, a few matters which are specific to Britain and may be unfamiliar to readers from other lands, and subjects of special interest – in brief notes following the text. But here, in this general introduction, it seems good to call attention to a few points at greater length.

In his 1939 Andrew Lang lecture *On Fairy-Stories* Tolkien criticized the 'flower-and-butterfly minuteness' of many depictions of fairies, citing in particular Michael Drayton's *Nymphidia* with the knight Pigwiggen riding on a 'frisky earwig' and 'making an assignation in a cowslip-flower'. But at the time of *Roverandom* he had not yet eschewed whimsical ideas such as moon-gnomes riding on rabbits and making pancakes out of snowflakes, and sea-fairies who drive in shell carriages harnessed to tiny fishes. Only some ten years earlier he had published a now famous piece of juvenilia, the poem 'Goblin Feet' (1915) in which the author hears 'tiny horns of enchanted leprechauns' and dwells on 'little robes' and 'little happy feet'; and as Tolkien once confessed, in the 1920s and 1930s he was 'still influenced by the convention that "fairy-stories" are naturally directed to children' (*Letters*, p. 297, draft of April 1959). Therefore he sometimes adopted common 'fairy-story' imagery and modes of expression: the playful, singing elves of Rivendell in *The Hobbit*, for example, and both in that work and (even more so) in

Roverandom, a prominent authorial (or parental) voice as narrator. Later Tolkien regretted having in any way 'written down' to his children, and wished especially that 'Goblin Feet' could be buried and forgotten. Meanwhile, the Fairies (later Elves) of his imagined 'Silmarillion' mythology stood tall and noble, with little trace of 'Pigwiggenry'.

Roverandom almost inevitably was drawn towards Tolkien's mythology (or *legendarium*), which by then he had developed for a decade or more and which remained for him a preoccupation. Several comparisons may be made between these works. The garden on the dark side of the moon in *Roverandom*, for example, closely recalls the Cottage of Lost Play in *The Book of Lost Tales,* the earliest prose treatment of the *legendarium*. In the latter children 'danced and played . . . , gathering flowers or chasing the golden bees and butterflies with embroidered wings' (*Part One* [published 1983], p. 19), while in the moon-garden they are 'dancing sleepily, walking dreamily, and talking to themselves. Some stirred as if just waking from deep sleep; some were already running wide awake and laughing: they were digging, gathering flowers, building tents and houses, chasing butterflies, kicking balls, climbing trees; and all were singing' (p. 42 below).

The Man-in-the-Moon will not say how the children arrive in his garden, but at one point Roverandom looks towards the earth and seems to see, 'faint and rather thin, long lines of small people sailing swiftly down' the moon-path (p. 46); and as the children come to the garden while asleep, it seems certain that Tolkien had in mind his already existing vision of the *Olórë Mallë* or Path of Dreams leading to the Cottage of Lost Play: 'slender bridges resting on the air and greyly gleaming as it were of silken mists lit by a thin moon', a path no man's eyes have beheld 'save in sweet slumbers in their heart's youth' (*The Book of Lost Tales, Part One*, p. 211).

The most intriguing connection between *Roverandom* and the mythology, however, occurs when the 'oldest whale', Uin, shows Roverandom 'the great Bay of Fairyland (as we call it) beyond the Magic Isles', and further off 'in the last West the Mountains of Elvenhome and the light of Faery upon the waves' and 'the city of the Elves on the green hill beneath the Mountains' (pp. 73–4). For this is precisely the geography of the West of the world in the 'Silmarillion', as that work existed in the 1920s and 1930s. The 'Mountains of Elvenhome' are the Mountains of Valinor in Aman, and the 'city of the Elves' is Tún – to use the name given it both at one time in the mythology and in the first text (only) of *Roverandom*. Uin too is drawn from *The Book of Lost Tales*, and although he is not here quite his namesake 'the mightiest and most ancient of whales' (*Part One*, p. 118), still he is able to carry Roverandom to within sight of the Western lands, which by this time in the development of the *legendarium* were hidden from mortal eyes behind darkness and perilous waters.

Uin says that he would 'catch it' if it was found out (presumably by the Valar, or Gods, who live in Valinor) that he had shown Aman to someone (even a dog!) from the 'Outer Lands' – that is, from Middle-earth, the world of mortals. In *Roverandom* that world in some ways is meant to be our own, with many real places mentioned by name. Roverandom himself 'after all was an English dog' (p. 51). But in other ways it is clearly not our earth: for one thing, it has edges over which waterfalls drop 'straight into space' (p. 21). This is not quite the earth depicted in the *legendarium* either, although it too is flat; but the moon of *Roverandom*, exactly like the one in *The Book of Lost Tales*, moves beneath the world when it is not in the sky above.

As more of Tolkien's works have been published in the quarter-century since his death, it has become clear that nearly all of his writings are interrelated, if only in small ways, and that each sheds a welcome light upon the others. *Roverandom* illustrates once again how the *legendarium* that was Tolkien's life-work influenced his storytelling, and it looks forward (or laterally) to writings on which *Roverandom* itself may have been an influence – especially to *The Hobbit*, whose composition (beginning possibly in 1927) was contemporaneous with the writing down and revision of *Roverandom*. Few readers of *The Hobbit* indeed will fail to notice (*inter alia*) similarities between Rover's fearsome flight with Mew to his cliff-side home and Bilbo's to the eagles' eyrie, and between the spiders Roverandom encounters on the moon and those of Mirkwood; that both the Great White Dragon and Smaug the dragon of Erebor have tender underbellies; and that the three crusty wizards in *Roverandom* – Artaxerxes, Psamathos, and the Man-in-the-Moon – each in his own way is a precursor of Gandalf.

*

Before proceeding to the text it remains only to say a few additional words about the pictures accompanying it. We have already discussed these illustrations at length in *J.R.R. Tolkien: Artist & Illustrator* (1995); but here, where they are at last printed together with the full text of the story, one can better appreciate their qualities and their shortcomings. They were not planned as illustrations for a printed book, and are not, in their subject matter, spaced equally throughout the story (in fact in the present book they have been placed according to the exigencies of production). Nor are they consistent even in style or media: two are in pen and ink, two in watercolour, and one chiefly in coloured pencil. Four are fully developed, the watercolours especially, while the fifth, the view of Rover arriving on the moon, is a much lesser work, with Rover, Mew, and the Man-in-the-Moon uncomfortably small.

In this drawing Tolkien was perhaps more interested in the tower and the (accurate) barren landscape, which however gives no hint of the lunar forests described in *Roverandom*. The earlier *Lunar Landscape* is more faithful to the text: it includes trees with blue leaves, and 'wide open spaces of pale blue and green where the tall pointed mountains threw their long shadows far across the floor' (p. 22). It presumably depicts the moment when Roverandom and the Man-in-the-Moon, returning from their visit to the dark side, see 'the world rise, a pale green and gold moon, huge and round above the shoulders of the Lunar Mountains' (p. 46). But here the world is clearly not flat: only the Americas are shown, and therefore England and the other earthly locations mentioned in the tale must be on the opposite side of a globe. The title *Lunar Landscape* is written on the work in an early form of Tolkien's Elvish script *tengwar*.

The White Dragon Pursues Roverandom & the Moondog is also faithful to the text, and has several points of interest besides the dragon and the two winged dogs. Above the titling are one of the moon-spiders and, probably, a dragonmoth; and in the sky again the earth is shown as a globe. When he came to illustrate *The Hobbit* Tolkien used the same dragon on his map *Wilderland*, and the same spider in his drawing of Mirkwood. 'Moondog' as in the title was used (variably with 'moon-dog') only in the earliest texts.

The splendid watercolour *The Gardens of the Merking's Palace* reveals the structure of 'pink and white stone' as if it were an aquarium decoration, perhaps with a hint of the Royal Pavilion at Brighton. Tolkien chose to show the palace and its gardens in all their beauty, rather than Roverandom making his fearful way up the path; probably we are meant to be seeing through his eyes. The whale Uin is in the upper left corner, much like the leviathan in one of Rudyard Kipling's illustrations for 'How the Whale Got His Throat' in his *Just So Stories* (1902). 'Merking' as in the title appeared only in the earliest texts, variably with 'mer-king' (the sole form in the final typescript). Tolkien was also inconsistent in his spelling of other *mer-* compounds, which in the present text we have regularized as hyphenated, excepting the familiar spellings *mermaid* (*mermaids*, *mermaidens*) and *mermen*.

The picture *House Where 'Rover' Began His Adventures as a 'Toy'*, no less accomplished a watercolour, is however a puzzle. Its title would suggest that it depicts the house where Rover first met Artaxerxes, though no indication is given in the text that this was on or near a farm. Also the glimpse of the sea in the background and the gull flying overhead would contradict the statement in the text that Rover 'had never either seen or smelt the sea' before he was taken to the beach by little boy Two, 'and the country village where he had been born was miles and miles from sound or snuff of it' (pp. 9–10). Nor can this be the little boys' father's house, which is described as being white and on a cliff with gardens running down to the sea. We are almost tempted to wonder if this picture was originally unconnected with the story, and then details, such as the gull, were added while it was being painted to give it relevance. The black and white dog at bottom left may be intended as a picture of Rover, and the black animal in front of him – like Rover, partially obscured by a pig – may be the cat, Tinker; but none of this is certain.

The text that follows is based on the latest version of *Roverandom*. Tolkien never fully edited the work for publication, and it cannot be doubted that he would have made a great many revisions and corrections, to make it more suitable for an audience apart from his immediate family, had it been accepted by Allen & Unwin as a successor to *The Hobbit*. In the event it was left with a number of errors and inconsistencies. When writing at speed Tolkien tended to be inconsistent in his manner of punctuation and capitalization; for *Roverandom* we have followed his (generally minimalist) practice where his intentions are clear, but have regularized punctuation marks and capitalization where it seemed necessary, and have corrected a few obvious typographical errors. With Christopher Tolkien's consent we have also amended a very small number of awkward phrases (retaining others); but for the most part the text is as its author left it.

For their advice and guidance in the making of this book we are especially grateful to Christopher Tolkien, whom we also thank for supplying the statement in his father's diary quoted on p. x; and to John Tolkien, who shared with us his memories of Filey in 1925. We would also like to acknowledge the assistance and encouragement of Priscilla and Joanna Tolkien; Douglas Anderson; David Doughan; Charles Elston; Michael Everson; Verlyn Flieger; Charles Fuqua; Christopher Gilson; Carl Hostetter; Alexei Kondratiev; John Rateliff; Arden Smith; Rayner Unwin; Patrick Wynne; David Brawn and Ali Bailey of HarperCollins; Judith Priestman and Colin Harris of the Bodleian Library, Oxford; and the staff of the Williams College Library, Williamstown, Massachusetts.

Christina Scull
Wayne G. Hammond

Roverandom

I

ONCE UPON A TIME there was a little dog, and his name was Rover. He was very small, and very young, or he would have known better; and he was very happy playing in the garden in the sunshine with a yellow ball, or he would never have done what he did.

Not every old man with ragged trousers is a bad old man: some are bone-and-bottle men, and have little dogs of their own; and some are gardeners; and a few, a very few, are wizards prowling round on a holiday looking for something to do. This one was a wizard, the one that now walked into the story. He came wandering up the garden-path in a ragged old coat, with an old pipe in his mouth, and an old green hat on his head. If Rover had not been so busy barking at the ball, he might have noticed the blue feather stuck in the back of the green hat, and then he would have suspected that the man was a wizard, as any other sensible little dog would; but he never saw the feather at all.

When the old man stooped down and picked up the ball – he was thinking of turning it into an orange, or even a bone or a piece of meat for Rover – Rover growled, and said:

'Put it down!' Without ever a 'please'.

Of course the wizard, being a wizard, understood perfectly, and he answered back again:

'Be quiet, silly!' Without ever a 'please'.

Then he put the ball in his pocket, just to tease the dog, and turned away. I am sorry to say that Rover immediately bit his trousers, and tore out quite a piece. Perhaps he also tore out a piece of the wizard. Anyway the old man suddenly turned round very angry and shouted:

'Idiot! Go and be a toy!'

After that the most peculiar things began to happen. Rover was only a little dog to begin with, but he suddenly felt very much smaller. The grass seemed to grow monstrously tall and wave far above his head; and a long way away through the grass, like the sun rising through the trees of a forest, he could see the huge yellow ball, where the wizard had thrown it down again. He heard the gate click as the old man went out, but he could not see him. He tried to bark, but only a little tiny noise came out, too small for ordinary people to hear; and I don't suppose even a dog would have noticed it.

So small had he become that I am sure, if a cat had come along just then, she would have thought Rover was a mouse, and would have eaten him. Tinker would. Tinker was the large black cat that lived in the same house.

At the very thought of Tinker, Rover began to feel thoroughly frightened; but cats were soon put right out of his mind. The garden about him suddenly vanished, and Rover felt himself whisked off, he didn't know where. When the rush was over, he found he was in the dark, lying against a lot of hard things; and there he lay, in a stuffy box by the feel of it, very uncomfortably for a long while. He had nothing to eat or drink; but worst of all, he found he could not move. At first he thought this was because he was packed so tight, but afterwards he discovered that in the daytime he could only move very little, and with a great effort, and then only when no one was looking. Only after midnight could he walk and wag his tail, and a bit stiffly at that. He had become a toy. And because he had not said 'please' to the wizard, now all day long he had to sit up and beg. He was fixed like that.

After what seemed a very long, dark time he tried once more to bark loud enough to make people hear. Then he tried to bite the other things in the box with him, stupid little toy animals, really only made of wood or lead, not enchanted real dogs like Rover. But it was no good; he could not bark or bite.

Suddenly someone came and took off the lid of the box, and let in the light.

'We had better put a few of these animals in the window this morning, Harry,' said a voice, and a hand came into the box. 'Where did this one come from?' said the voice, as the hand took hold of Rover. 'I don't remember seeing this one before. It's no business in the threepenny box, I'm sure. Did you ever see anything so real-looking? Look at its fur and its eyes!'

'Mark him sixpence,' said Harry, 'and put him in the front of the window!'

There in the front of the window in the hot sun poor little Rover had to sit all the morning, and all the afternoon, till nearly tea-time; and all the while he had to sit up and pretend to beg, though really in his inside he was very angry indeed.

'I'll run away from the very first people that buy me,' he said to the other toys. 'I'm real. I'm not a toy, and I won't be a toy! But I wish someone would come and buy me quick. I hate this shop, and I can't move all stuck up in the window like this.'

'What do you want to move for?' said the other toys. 'We don't. It's more comfortable standing still thinking of nothing. The more you rest, the longer you live. So just shut up! We can't sleep while you're talking, and there are hard times in rough nurseries in front of some of us.'

They would not say any more, so poor Rover had no one at all to talk to, and he was very miserable, and very sorry he had bitten the wizard's trousers.

I could not say whether it was the wizard or not who sent the mother to take the little dog away from the shop. Anyway, just when Rover was feeling his miserablest, into the shop she walked with a shopping-basket. She had seen Rover through the window, and thought what a nice little dog he would be for her boy. She had three boys, and one was particularly fond of little dogs, especially of little black and white dogs. So she bought Rover, and he was screwed up in paper and put in her basket among the things she had been buying for tea.

Rover soon managed to wriggle his head out of the paper. He smelt cake. But he found he could not get at it; and right down there among the paper bags he growled a little toy growl. Only the shrimps heard him, and they asked him what was the matter. He told them all about it, and expected them to be very sorry for him, but they only said:

'How would you like to be boiled? Have you ever been boiled?'

'No! I have never been boiled, as far as I remember,' said Rover, 'though I have sometimes been bathed, and that is not particularly nice. But I expect boiling isn't half as bad as being bewitched.'

'Then you have certainly never been boiled,' they answered. 'You know nothing about it. It's the very worst thing that could happen to anyone – we are still red with rage at the very idea.'

Rover did not like the shrimps, so he said: 'Never mind, they will soon eat you up, and I shall sit and watch them!'

After that the shrimps had no more to say to him, and he was left to lie and wonder what sort of people had bought him.

He soon found out. He was carried to a house, and the basket was set down on a table, and all the parcels were taken out. The shrimps were taken off to the larder, but Rover was given straight away to the little boy he had been bought for, who took him into the nursery and talked to him.

Rover would have liked the little boy, if he had not been too angry to listen to what he was saying to him. The little boy barked at him in the best dog-language he could manage (he was rather good at it), but Rover never tried to answer. All the time he was thinking he had said he would run away from the first people that bought him, and he was wondering how he could do it; and all the time he had to sit up and pretend to beg, while the little boy patted him and pushed him about, over the table and along the floor.

At last night came, and the little boy went to bed; and Rover was put on a chair by the bedside, still begging until it was quite dark. The blind was down; but outside the moon rose up out of the sea, and laid the silver path across the waters that is the way to places at the edge of the world and beyond, for those that can walk on it. The father and mother and the three little boys lived close by the sea in a white house that looked right out over the waves to nowhere.

When the little boys were asleep, Rover stretched his tired, stiff legs and gave a little bark that nobody heard except an old wicked spider up a corner. Then he jumped from the chair to the bed, and from the bed he tumbled off onto the carpet; and then he ran away out of the room and down the stairs and all over the house.

Although he was very pleased to be able to move again, and having once been real and properly alive he could jump and run a good deal better than most toys at night, he found it very difficult and dangerous getting about. He was now so small that going downstairs was almost like jumping off walls; and getting upstairs again was very tiring and awkward indeed. And it was all no use. He found all the doors shut and locked, of course; and there was not a crack or a hole by which he could creep out. So poor Rover could not run away that night, and morning found a very tired little dog sitting up and pretending to beg on the chair, just where he had been left.

The two older boys used to get up, when it was fine, and run along the sands before their breakfast. That morning when they woke and pulled up the blind, they saw the sun jumping out of the sea, all fiery-red with clouds about his head, as if he had had a cold bathe and was drying himself with towels. They were soon up and dressed; and off they went down the cliff and onto the shore for a walk – and Rover went with them.

Just as little boy Two (to whom Rover belonged) was leaving the bedroom, he saw Rover sitting on the chest-of-drawers where he had put him while he was dressing. 'He is begging to go out!' he said, and put him in his trouser-pocket.

But Rover was not begging to go out, and certainly not in a trouser-pocket. He wanted to rest and get ready for the night again; for he thought that this time he might find a way out and escape, and wander away and away, until he came back to his home and his garden and his yellow ball on the lawn. He had a sort of idea that if once he could get back to the lawn, it might come all right: the enchantment might break, or he might wake up and find it had all been a dream. So, as the little boys scrambled down the cliff-path and galloped along the sands, he tried to bark and struggle and wriggle in the pocket. Try how he would, he could only move a very little, even though he was hidden and no one could see him. Still he did what he could, and luck helped him. There was a handkerchief in the pocket, all crumpled and bundled up, so that Rover was not very deep down, and what with his efforts and the galloping of his master, before long he had managed to poke out his nose and have a sniff round.

Very surprised he was, too, at what he smelt and what he saw. He had never either seen or smelt the sea before, and the country village where he had been born was miles and miles from sound or snuff of it.

Suddenly, as he was leaning out, a great big bird, all white and grey, went sweeping by just over the heads of the boys, making a noise like a great cat on wings. Rover was so startled that he fell right out of the pocket onto the soft sand, and no one heard him. The great bird flew on and away, never noticing his tiny barks, and the little boys walked on and on along the sands, and never thought about him at all.

At first Rover was very pleased with himself.

'I've run away! I've run away!' he barked, toy barking that only other toys could have heard, and there were none to listen. Then he rolled over and lay in the clean dry sand that was still cool from lying out all night under the stars.

But when the little boys went by on their way home, and never noticed him, and he was left all alone on the empty shore, he was not quite so pleased. The shore was deserted except by the gulls. Beside the marks of their claws on the sand the only other footprints to be seen were the tracks of the little boys' feet. That morning they had gone for their walk on a very lonely part of the beach that they seldom visited. Indeed it was not often that anyone went there; for though the sand was clean and yellow, and the shingle white, and the sea blue with silver foam in a little cove under the grey cliffs, there was a queer feeling there, except just at early morning when the sun was new. People said that strange things came there, sometimes even in the afternoon; and by the evening the place was full of mermen and mermaidens, not to speak of the smaller sea-goblins that rode their small sea-horses with bridles of green weed right up to the cliffs and left them lying in the foam at the edge of the water.

Now the reason of all this queerness was simple: the oldest of all the sand-sorcerers lived in that cove, *Psamathists* as the sea-people call them in their splashing language. Psamathos Psamathides was this one's name, or so he said, and a great fuss he made about the proper pronunciation. But he was a wise old thing, and all sorts of strange folk came to see him; for he was an excellent magician, and very kindly (to the right people) into the bargain, if a bit crusty on the surface. The mer-folk used to laugh over his jokes for weeks after one of his midnight parties. But it was not easy to find him in the daytime. He liked to lie buried in the warm sand when the sun was shining, so that not more than the tip of one of his long ears stuck out; and even if both of his ears were showing, most people like you and me would have taken them for bits of stick.

It is possible that old Psamathos knew all about Rover. He certainly knew the old wizard who had enchanted him; for magicians and wizards are few and far between, and they know one another very well, and keep an eye on one another's doings too, not always being the best of friends in private life. At any rate there was Rover lying in the soft sand and beginning to feel very lonely and rather queer, and there was Psamathos, though Rover did not see him, peeping at him out of a pile of sand that the mermaids had made for him the night before.

But the sand-sorcerer said nothing. And Rover said nothing. And breakfast-time went by, and the sun got high and hot. Rover looked at the sea, which sounded cool, and then he got a horrible fright. At first he thought that the sand must have got into his eyes, but soon he saw that there could be no mistake: the sea was moving nearer and nearer, and swallowing up more and more sand; and the waves were getting bigger and bigger and more foamy all the time.

The tide was coming in, and Rover was lying just below the high-water mark, but he did not know anything about that. He grew more and more terrified as he watched, and thought of the splashing waves coming right up to the cliffs and washing him away into the foaming sea (far worse than any soapy bathing-tub), still miserably begging.

That is indeed what might have happened to him; but it did not. I dare say Psamathos had something to do with it; at any rate I imagine that the wizard's spell was not so strong in that queer cove, so close to the residence of another magician. Certainly when the sea had come very near, and Rover was nearly bursting with fright as he struggled to roll a bit further up the beach, he suddenly found he could move.

His size was not changed, but he was no longer a toy. He could move quickly and properly with all his legs, daytime though it still was. He need not beg any more, and he could run over the sands where they were harder; and he could bark – not toy barks, but real sharp little fairy-dog barks equal to his fairy-dog size. He was so delighted, and he barked so loud, that if you had been there, you would have heard him then, clear and far-away-like, like the echo of a sheep-dog coming down the wind in the hills.

And then the sand-sorcerer suddenly stuck his head out of the sand. He certainly was ugly, and about as big as a very large dog; but to Rover in his enchanted size he looked hideous and monstrous. Rover sat down and stopped barking at once.

'What are you making such a noise about, little dog?' said Psamathos Psamathides. 'This is my time for sleep!'

As a matter of fact all times were times for him to go to sleep, unless something was going on which amused him, such as a dance of the mermaids in the cove (at his invitation). In that case he got out of the sand and sat on a rock to see the fun. Mermaids may be very graceful in the water, but when they tried to dance on their tails on the shore, Psamathos thought them comical.

'This is my time for sleep!' he said again, when Rover did not answer. Still Rover said nothing, and only wagged his tail apologetically.

'Do you know who I am?' he asked. 'I am Psamathos Psamathides, the chief of all the Psamathists!' He said this several times very proudly, pronouncing every letter, and with every *P* he blew a cloud of sand down his nose.

Rover was nearly buried in it, and he sat there looking so frightened and so unhappy that the sand-sorcerer took pity on him. In fact he suddenly stopped looking fierce and burst out laughing:

'You are a funny little dog, Little Dog! Indeed I don't remember ever having seen another little dog that was quite such a little dog, Little Dog!'

And then he laughed again, and after that he suddenly looked solemn.

'Have you been having any quarrels with wizards lately?' he asked almost in a whisper; and he shut one eye, and looked so friendly and so knowing out of the other one that Rover told him all about it. It was probably quite unnecessary, for Psamathos, as I told you, probably knew about it beforehand; still Rover felt all the better for talking to someone who appeared to understand and had more sense than mere toys.

'It was a wizard all right,' said the sorcerer, when Rover had finished his tale. 'Old Artaxerxes, I should think from your description. He comes from Persia. But he lost his way one day, as even the best wizards sometimes do (unless they always stay at home like me), and the first person he met on the road went and put him on the way to Pershore instead. He has lived in those parts, except on holidays, ever since. They say he is a nimble plum-gatherer for an old man – two thousand, if he is a day – and extremely fond of cider. But that's neither here nor there.' By which Psamathos meant that he was getting away from what he wanted to say. 'The point is, what can I do for you?'

'I don't know,' said Rover.

'Do you want to go home? I am afraid I can't make you your proper size, at least not without asking Artaxerxes' permission first, as I don't want to quarrel with him at the moment. But I think I might venture to send you home. After all, Artaxerxes can always send you back again, if he wants to. Though of course he might send you somewhere much worse than a toyshop next time, if he was really annoyed.'

Rover did not like the sound of this at all, and he ventured to say that if he went back home so small, he might not be recognized, except by Tinker the cat; and he did not very much want to be recognized by Tinker in his present state.

'Very well!' said Psamathos. 'We must think of something else. In the meantime, as you are real again, would you like something to eat?'

Before Rover had time to say 'Yes, please! YES! PLEASE!' there appeared on the sands in front of him a little plate with bread and gravy and two tiny bones of just the right size, and a little drinking-bowl full of water with DRINK PUPPY DRINK written round it in small blue letters. He ate and drank all there was before he asked: 'How did you do that? – Thank you!'

He suddenly thought of adding the 'thank you', as wizards and people of that sort seemed rather touchy folk. Psamathos only smiled; so Rover lay down on the hot sand and went to sleep, and dreamed of bones, and of chasing cats up plum-trees only to see them change into wizards with green hats who threw enormous plums like marrows at him. And the wind blew gently all the time, and buried him almost over his head in blown sand.

That is why the little boys never found him, although they came down into the cove specially to look for him, as soon as little boy Two found he was lost. Their father was with them this time; and when they had looked and looked till the sun began to get low and tea-timish, he took them back home and would not stay any longer: he knew too many queer things about that place. Little boy Two had to be content for some time after that with an ordinary threepenny toy dog (from the same shop); but somehow, though he had only had him such a short while, he did not forget his little begging-dog.

At the moment, however, you can think of him sitting down very mournful to his tea, without any dog at all; while far away inland the old lady who had kept Rover and spoiled him, when he was an ordinary, proper-sized animal, was just writing out an advertisement for a lost puppy – 'white with black ears, and answers to the name of Rover'; and while Rover himself slept away on the sands, and Psamathos dozed close by with his short arms folded on his fat tummy.

2

When Rover woke up, the sun was very low; the shadow of the cliffs was right across the sands, and Psamathos was nowhere to be seen. A large seagull was standing close by looking at him, and for a moment Rover was afraid that he might be going to eat him.

But the seagull said: 'Good evening! I have waited a long time for you to wake up. Psamathos said that you would wake about tea-time, but it is long past that now.'

'Please, what are you waiting for me for, Mr Bird?' asked Rover very politely.

'My name is Mew,' said the seagull, 'and I'm waiting to take you away, as soon as the moon rises, along the moon's path. But we have one or two things to do before that. Get up on my back and see how you like flying!'

Rover did not like it at all at first. It was all right while Mew was close to the ground, gliding smoothly along with his wings stretched out stiff and still; but when he shot up into the air, or turned sharp from side to side, sloping a different way each time, or stooped sudden and steep, as if he was going to dive into the sea, then the little dog, with the wind whistling in his ears, wished he was safe down on the earth again.

He said so several times, but all that Mew would answer was: 'Hold on! We haven't begun yet!'

They had been flying about like this for a little, and Rover had just begun to get used to it, and rather tired of it, when suddenly 'We're off!' cried Mew; and Rover very nearly was off. For Mew rose like a rocket steeply into the air, and then set off at a great pace straight down the wind. Soon they were so high that Rover could see, far away and right over the land, the sun going down behind dark hills. They were making for some very tall black cliffs of sheer rock, too sheer for anyone to climb. At the bottom the sea was splashing and sucking at their feet, and nothing grew on their faces, yet they were covered with white things, pale in the dusk. Hundreds of sea-birds were sitting there on narrow ledges, sometimes talking mournfully together, sometimes saying nothing, and sometimes slipping suddenly from their perches to swoop and curve in the air, before diving down to the sea far below where the waves looked like little wrinkles.

This was where Mew lived, and he had several people to see, including the oldest and most important of all the Blackbacked Gulls, and messages to collect before he set out. So he set Rover down on one of the narrow ledges, much narrower than a doorstep, and told him to wait there and not to fall off.

You may be sure that Rover took care not to fall off, and that with a stiff sideways wind blowing he did not like the feeling of it at all, crouching as close as he could against the face of the cliff, and whimpering. It was altogether a very nasty place for a bewitched and worried little dog to be in.

At last the sunlight faded out of the sky entirely, and a mist was on the sea, and the first stars showed in the gathering dark. Then above the mist, far out across the sea, the moon rose round and yellow and began to lay its shining path on the water.

Soon after, Mew came back and picked up Rover, who had begun to shiver miserably. The bird's feathers seemed warm and comfortable after the cold ledge on the cliff, and he snuggled in as close as he could. Then Mew leapt into the air far above the sea, and all the other gulls sprang off their ledges, and cried and wailed good-bye to them, as off they sped along the moon's path that now stretched straight from the shore to the dark edge of nowhere.

Rover did not know in the least where the moon's path led to, and at present he was much too frightened and excited to ask, and anyway he was beginning to get used to extraordinary things happening to him.

As they flew along above the silver shimmer on the sea, the moon rose higher and grew whiter and more bright, till no stars dared stay anywhere near it, and it was left shining all alone in the eastern sky. No doubt Mew was going by Psamathos' orders to where Psamathos wanted him to go, and no doubt Psamathos helped Mew with magic, for he certainly flew faster and straighter than even the great gulls ordinarily fly, even straight down the wind when they are in a hurry. Yet it was ages before Rover saw anything except the moonlight and the sea below; and all the time the moon got bigger and bigger, and the air got colder and colder.

Suddenly on the edge of the sea he saw a dark thing, and it grew as they flew towards it, until he could see that it was an island. Over the water and up to them came the sound of a tremendous barking, a noise made up of all the different kinds and sizes of barks there are: yaps and yelps, and yammers and yowls, growling and grizzling, whickering and whining, snickering and snarling, mumping and moaning, and the most enormous baying, like a giant bloodhound in the backyard of an ogre. All Rover's fur round his neck suddenly became very real again, and stood up stiff as bristles; and he thought he would like to go down and quarrel with all the dogs there at once – until he remembered how small he was.

'That's the Isle of Dogs,' said Mew, 'or rather the Isle of Lost Dogs, where all the lost dogs go that are deserving or lucky. It isn't a bad place, I'm told, for dogs; and they can make as much noise as they like without anyone telling them to be quiet or throwing anything at them. They have a beautiful concert, all barking together their favourite noises, whenever the moon shines bright. They tell me there are bone-trees there, too, with fruit like juicy meat-bones that drops off the trees when it's ripe. No! We are not going there just now! You see, you can't be called exactly a dog, though you are no longer quite a toy. In fact Psamathos was rather puzzled, I believe, to know what to do with you, when you said you didn't want to go home.'

'Where are we going to, then?' asked Rover. He was disappointed at not having a closer look at the Isle of Dogs, after he heard of the bone-trees.

'Straight up the moon's path to the edge of the world, and then over the edge and onto the moon. That's what old Psamathos said.'

Rover did not like the idea of going over the edge of the world at all, and the moon looked a cold sort of place. 'Why to the moon?' he asked. 'There are lots of places on the world I have never been to. I never heard of there being bones in the moon, or even dogs.'

'There is at least one dog, for the Man-in-the-Moon keeps one; and since he is a decent old fellow, as well as the greatest of all the magicians, there are sure to be bones for the dog, and probably for visitors. As for why you are being sent there, I dare say you will find that out in good time, if you keep your wits about you and don't waste time grumbling. I think it is very kind of Psamathos to bother about you at all; in fact I don't understand why he does. It isn't like him to do things without a good big reason – and you don't seem good or big.'

'Thank you,' said Rover, feeling crushed. 'It is very kind of all these wizards to trouble themselves about me, I am sure, though it is rather upsetting. You never know what will happen next, when once you get mixed up with wizards and their friends.'

'It is very much better luck than any yapping little pet puppy-dog deserves,' said the seagull, and after that they had no more conversation for a long while.

The moon got bigger and brighter, and the world below got darker and farther off. At last, all of a sudden, the world came to an end, and Rover could see the stars shining up out of the blackness underneath. Far down he could see the white spray in the moonlight where waterfalls fell over the world's edge and dropped straight into space. It made him feel most uncomfortably giddy, and he nestled into Mew's feathers and shut his eyes for a long, long time.

When he opened them again the moon was all laid out below them, a new white world shining like snow, with wide open spaces of pale blue and green where the tall pointed mountains threw their long shadows far across the floor.

On top of one of the tallest of these, one so tall that it seemed to stab up towards them as Mew swept down, Rover could see a white tower. It was white with pink and pale green lines in it, shimmering as if the tower were built of millions of seashells still wet with foam and gleaming; and the tower stood on the edge of a white precipice, white as a cliff of chalk, but shining with moonlight more brightly than a pane of glass far away on a cloudless night.

There was no path down that cliff, as far as Rover could see; but that did not matter at the moment, for Mew was sailing swiftly down, and soon he settled right on the roof of the tower, at a dizzy height above the moon-world that made the cliffs by the sea where Mew lived seem low and safe.

To Rover's great surprise a little door in the roof immediately opened close beside them, and an old man with a long silvery beard popped his head out.

'Not bad going, that!' he said. 'I've been timing you ever since you passed over the edge – a thousand miles a minute, I should reckon. You are in a hurry this morning! I'm glad you didn't bump into my dog. Where in the moon has he got to now, I wonder?'

He drew out an enormously long telescope and put it to one eye.

'There he is! There he is!' he shouted. 'Worrying the moonbeams again, drat him! Come down, sir! Come down, sir!' he called up into the air, and then began to whistle a long clear silver note.

Rover looked up into the air, thinking that this funny old man must be quite mad to whistle to his dog up in the sky; but to his astonishment he saw far up above the tower a little white dog on white wings chasing things that looked like transparent butterflies.

'Rover! Rover!' called the old man; and just as our Rover jumped up on Mew's back to say 'Here I am!' – without waiting to wonder how the old man knew his name – he saw the little flying dog dive straight down out of the sky and settle on the old man's shoulders.

Then he realised that the Man-in-the-Moon's dog must also be called Rover. He was not at all pleased, but as nobody took any notice of him, he sat down again and began to growl to himself.

The Man-in-the-Moon's Rover had good ears, and he at once jumped onto the roof of the tower and began to bark like mad; and then he sat down and growled: 'Who brought that other dog here?'

'What other dog?' said the Man.

'That silly little puppy on the seagull's back,' said the moon-dog.

Then, of course, Rover jumped up again and barked his loudest: 'Silly little puppy yourself! Who said that you could call yourself Rover, a thing more like a cat or a bat than a dog?' From which you can see that they were going to be very friendly before long. That is the way, anyhow, that little dogs usually talk to strangers of their own kind.

'O fly away, you two! And stop making such a noise! I want to talk to the postman,' said the Man.

'Come on, tiny tot!' said the moon-dog; and then Rover remembered what a tiny tot he was, even beside the moon-dog who was only small, and instead of barking something rude he only said: 'I would like to, if only I had some wings and knew how to fly.'

'Wings?' said the Man-in-the-Moon. 'That's easy! Have a pair and be off!'

Mew laughed, and actually threw him off his back, right over the edge of the tower's roof! But Rover had only gasped once, and had only begun to imagine himself falling and falling down like a stone onto the white rocks in the valley miles below, when he discovered that he had got a beautiful pair of white wings with black spots (to match himself). All the same, he had fallen a long way before he could stop, as he wasn't used to wings. It took him a little while to get really used to them, though long before the Man had finished talking to Mew he was already trying to chase the moon-dog round the tower. He was just beginning to get tired by these first efforts, when the moon-dog dived down to the mountain-top and settled at the edge of the precipice at the foot of the walls. Rover went down after him, nd soon they were sitting side by side, taking breath with their tongues hanging out.

'So you are called Rover after me?' said the moon-dog.

'Not after you,' said our Rover. 'I'm sure my mistress had never heard of you when she gave me my name.'

'That doesn't matter. I was the first dog that was ever called Rover, thousands of years ago – so you must have been called Rover after me! I *was* a Rover too! I never would stop anywhere, or belong to anyone before I came here. I did nothing but run away from the time I was a puppy; and I kept on running and roving until one fine morning – a very fine morning, with the sun in my eyes – I fell over the world's edge chasing a butterfly.

'A nasty sensation, I can tell you! Luckily the moon was just passing under the world at the moment, and after a terrible time falling right through clouds, and bumping into shooting stars, and that sort of thing, I tumbled onto it. Slap into one of the enormous silver nets that the giant grey spiders here spin from mountain to mountain I fell, and the spider was just coming down his ladder to pickle me and carry me off to his larder, when the Man-in-the-Moon appeared.

'He sees absolutely everything that happens on this side of the moon with that telescope of his. The spiders are afraid of him, because he only lets them alone if they spin silver threads and ropes for him. He more than suspects that they catch his moonbeams – and that he won't allow – though they pretend to live only on dragonmoths and shadowbats. He found moonbeams' wings in that spider's larder, and he turned him into a lump of stone, as quick as kiss your hand. Then he picked me up and patted me, and said: "That was a nasty drop! You had better have a pair of wings to prevent any more accidents – now fly off and amuse yourself! Don't worry the moonbeams, and don't kill my white rabbits! And come home when you feel hungry; the window is usually open on the roof!"

'I thought he was a decent sort, but rather mad. But don't you make that mistake – about his being mad,

I mean. I daren't really hurt his moonbeams or his rabbits. He can turn you into dreadfully uncomfortable shapes. Now tell me why you came with the postman!'

'The postman?' said Rover.

'Yes, Mew, the old sand-sorcerer's postman, of course,' said the moon-dog.

Rover had hardly finished telling the tale of his adventures when they heard the Man whistling. Up they shot to the roof. There the old man was sitting with his legs dangling over the ledge, throwing envelopes away as fast as he opened the letters. The wind took them whirling off into the sky, and Mew flew after them and caught them and put them back into a little bag.

'I've just been reading about you, Roverandom, my dog,' he said. '(Roverandom I call you, and Roverandom you'll have to be; can't have two Rovers about here.) And I quite agree with my friend Samathos (I'm not going to put in any ridiculous *P* to please him) that you had better stop here for a little while. I have also got a letter from Artaxerxes, if you know who that is, and even if you don't, telling me to send you straight back. He seems mighty annoyed with you for running away, and with Samathos for helping you. But we won't bother about him; and neither need you, as long as you stay here.

'Now fly off and amuse yourself. Don't worry the moonbeams, and don't kill my white rabbits, and come home when you are hungry! The window on the roof is usually open. Good-bye!'

He vanished immediately into thin air; and anybody who has never been there will tell you how extremely thin the moon-air is.

'Well, good-bye, Roverandom!' said Mew. 'I hope you enjoy making trouble among the wizards. Farewell for the present. Don't kill the white rabbits, and all will yet be well, and you will get home safe – whether you want to or not.'

Then Mew flew off at such a pace that before you could say 'whizz!' he was a dot in the sky, and then had vanished. Rover was now not only turned into toy-size, but his name had been altered, and he was left all alone on the moon – all alone except for the Man-in-the-Moon and his dog.

Roverandom – as we had better call him too, for the present, to avoid confusion – didn't mind. His new wings were great fun, and the moon turned out to be a remarkably interesting place, so that he forgot to ponder any more why Psamathos had sent him there. It was a long time before he found out.

In the meanwhile he had all sorts of adventures, by himself and with the moon-Rover. He didn't often fly about in the air far from the tower; for in the moon, and especially on the white side, the insects are very large and fierce, and often so pale and so transparent and so silent that you hardly hear or see them coming. The moonbeams only shine and flutter, and Roverandom was not frightened of them; the big white dragon-moths with fiery eyes were much more alarming; and there were sword-flies, and glass-beetles with jaws like steel-traps, and pale unicornets with stings like spears, and fifty-seven varieties of spiders ready to eat anything they could catch. And worse than the insects were the shadowbats.

Roverandom did what the birds do on that side of the moon: he flew very little except near at home, or in open spaces with a good view all round, and far from insect hiding-places; and he walked about very quietly, especially in the woods. Most things there went about very quietly, and the birds seldom even twittered. What sounds there were, were made chiefly by the plants. The flowers – the whitebells, the fairbells and the silverbells, the tinklebells and the ringaroses; the rhymeroyals and the pennywhistles, the tintrumpets and the creamhorns (a very pale cream), and many others with untranslatable names – made tunes all day long. And the feather-grasses and the ferns – fairy-fiddlestrings, polyphonies, and brasstongues, and the cracken in the woods – and all the reeds by the milk-white ponds, they kept up the music, softly, even in the night. In fact there was always a faint thin music going on.

But the birds were silent; and very tiny most of them were, hopping about in the grey grass beneath the trees, dodging the flies and the swooping flutterbies; and many of them had lost their wings or forgotten how to use them. Roverandom used to startle them in their little ground-nests, as he stalked quietly through the pale grass, hunting the little white mice, or snuffing after grey squirrels on the edges of the woods.

The woods were filled with silverbells all ringing softly together when he first saw them. The tall black trunks stood straight up, high as churches, out of the silver carpet, and they were roofed with pale blue leaves that never fell; so that not even the longest telescope on earth has ever seen those tall trunks or the silverbells beneath them. Later in the year the trees all burst together into pale golden blossoms; and since the woods of the moon are nearly endless, no doubt that alters the look of the moon from below on the world.

But you must not imagine that all of Roverandom's time was spent creeping about like that. After all, the dogs knew that the Man's eye was on them, and they did a good many adventurous things and had a great deal of fun. Sometimes they wandered off together for miles and miles, and forgot to go back to the tower for days. Once or twice they went up into the mountains far away, till looking back they could see the moon-tower only as a shining needle in the distance; and they sat on the white rocks and watched the tiny sheep (no bigger than the Man-in-the-Moon's Rover) wandering in herds over the hillsides. Every sheep carried a golden bell, and every bell rang each time each sheep moved a foot forward to get a fresh mouthful of grey grass; and all the bells rang in tune, and all the sheep shone like snow, and no one ever worried them. The Rovers were much too well brought-up (and afraid of the Man) to do so, and there were no other dogs in all the moon, nor cows, nor horses, nor lions, nor tigers, nor wolves; in fact nothing larger on four feet than rabbits and squirrels (and toy-sized at that), except just occasionally to be seen standing solemnly in thought an enormous white elephant almost as big as a donkey. I haven't mentioned the dragons, because they don't come into the story just yet, and anyway they lived a very long way off, far from the tower, being all very afraid of the Man-in-the-Moon, except one (and even he was half-afraid).

Whenever the dogs did go back to the tower and fly in at the window, they always found their dinner just ready, as if they had arranged the time; but they seldom saw or heard the Man about. He had a workshop down in the cellars, and clouds of white steam and grey mist used to come up the stairs and float away out of the upper windows.

'What does he do with himself all day?' said Roverandom to Rover.

'Do?' said the moon-dog. 'O he's always pretty busy – though he seems busier than I have seen him for a long time, since you arrived. Making dreams, I believe.'

'What does he make dreams for?'

'O! for the other side of the moon. No one has dreams on this side; the dreamers all go round to the back.'

Roverandom sat down and scratched; he didn't think the explanation explained. The moon-dog would not tell him any more all the same: and if you ask me, I don't think he knew much about it.

However, something happened soon after that, that put such questions out of Roverandom's mind altogether for a while. The two dogs went and had a very exciting adventure, much too exciting while it lasted; but that was their own fault. They went away for several days, much farther than they had ever been before since Roverandom came; and they did not bother to think where they were going. In fact they went and lost themselves, and mistaking the way got farther and farther from the tower when they thought they were getting back. The moon-dog said he had roamed all over the white side of the moon and knew it all by heart (he was very apt to exaggerate), but eventually he had to admit that the country seemed a bit strange.

'I'm afraid it's a very long time since I came here,' he said, 'and I'm beginning to forget it a bit.'

As a matter of fact he had never been there before at all. Unawares they had wandered too near to the shadowy edge of the dark side, where all sorts of half-forgotten things linger, and paths and memories get confused. Just when they felt sure that at last they were on the right way home, they were surprised to find some tall mountains rising before them, silent, bare, and ominous; and these the moon-dog made no pretence of ever having seen before. They were grey, not white, and looked as if they were made of old cold ashes; and long dim valleys lay among them, without a sign of life.

Then it began to snow. It often does snow in the moon, but the snow (as they call it) is usually nice and warm, and quite dry, and turns into fine white sand and all blows away. This was more like our sort. It was wet and cold; and it was dirty.

'It makes me homesick,' said the moon-dog. 'It's just like the stuff that used to fall in the town where I was a puppy – on the world, you know. O! the chimneys there, tall as moon-trees; and the black smoke; and the red furnace fires! I get a bit tired of white at times. It's very difficult to get really dirty on the moon.'

This rather shows up the moon-dog's low tastes; and as there were no such towns on the world hundreds of years ago, you can also see that he had exaggerated the length of time since he fell over the edge a very great deal too. However, just at that moment, a specially large and dirty flake hit him in the left eye, and he changed his mind.

'I think this stuff has missed its way and fallen off the beastly old world,' he said. 'Rat and rabbit it! And we seem to have missed our way altogether, too. Bat and bother it! Let's find a hole to creep in!'

It took some time to find a hole of any sort, and they were very wet and cold before they did: in fact so miserable that they took the first shelter they came to, and no precautions – which are the first things you ought to take in unfamiliar places on the edge of the moon. The shelter they crawled into was not a hole but a cave, and a very large cave too; it was dark but it was dry.

'This is nice and warm,' said the moon-dog, and he closed his eyes and went off into a doze almost immediately.

'Ow!' he yelped not long afterwards, waking straight up dog-fashion out of a comfortable dream. 'Much too warm!'

He jumped up. He could hear little Roverandom barking away further inside the cave, and when he went to see what was up, he saw a trickle of fire creeping along the floor towards them. He did not feel homesick for red furnaces just then; and he seized little Roverandom by the back of his little neck, and bolted out of the cave as quick as lightning, and flew up to a peak of stone just outside.

There the two sat in the snow shivering and watching; which was very silly of them. They ought to have flown off home, or anywhere, faster than the wind. The moon-dog did not know everything about the moon, as you see, or he would have known that this was the lair of the Great White Dragon – the one that was only half-afraid of the Man (and scarcely that when he was angry). The Man himself was a bit bothered by this dragon. 'That dratted creature' was what he called him, when he referred to him at all.

All the white dragons originally come from the moon, as you probably know; but this one had been to the world and back, so he had learned a thing or two. He fought the Red Dragon in Caerdragon in Merlin's time, as you will find in all the more up-to-date history books; after which the other dragon was Very Red. Later he did lots more damage in the Three Islands, and went to live on the top of Snowdon for a time. People did not bother to climb up while that lasted – except for one man, and the dragon caught him drinking out of a bottle. That man finished in such a hurry that he left the bottle on the top, and his example has been followed by many people since. A long time since, and not until the dragon had flown off to Gwynfa, some time after King Arthur's disappearance, at a time when dragons' tails were esteemed a great delicacy by the Saxon Kings.

Gwynfa is not so far from the world's edge, and it is an easy flight from there to the moon for a dragon so titanic and so enormously bad as this one had become. He now lived on the moon's edge; for he was not quite sure how much the Man-in-the-Moon could do with his spells and contrivances. All the same, he actually dared at times to interfere with the colour-scheme. Sometimes he let real red and green flames out of his cave when he was having a dragon-feast or was in a tantrum; and clouds of smoke were frequent. Once or twice he had been known to turn the whole moon red, or put it out altogether. On such uncomfortable occasions the Man-in-the-Moon shut himself up (and his dog), and all he said was 'That dratted creature again'. He never explained what creature, or where he lived; he simply went down into the cellars, uncorked his best spells, and got things cleared up as quick as possible.

Now you know all about it; and if the dogs had known half as much they would never have stopped there. But stop they did, at least as long as it has taken me to explain about the White Dragon, and by that time the whole of him, white with green eyes, and leaking green fire at every joint, and snorting black smoke like a steamer, had come out of the cave. Then he let off the most awful bellow. The mountains rocked and echoed, and the snow dried up; avalanches tumbled down, and waterfalls stood still.

That dragon had wings, like the sails that ships had when they still were ships and not steam-engines; and he did not disdain to kill anything from a mouse to an emperor's daughter. He meant to kill those two dogs; and he told them so several times before he got up into the air. That was *his* mistake. They both whizzed off their rock like rockets, and went away down the wind at a pace that Mew himself would have been proud of. The dragon came after them, flapping like a flapdragon and snapping like a snapdragon, knocking the tops of mountains off, and setting all the sheep-bells ringing like a town on fire. (Now you see why they all had bells.)

Very luckily, down the wind was the right direction. Also a most stupendous rocket went up from the tower as soon as the bells got frantic. It could be seen all over the moon like a golden umbrella bursting into a thousand silver tassels, and it caused an unpredicted fall of shooting stars on the world not long after. If it was a guide to the poor dogs, it was also meant as a warning to the dragon; but he had got far too much steam up to take any notice.

So the chase went fiercely on. If you have ever seen a bird chasing a butterfly, and if you can imagine a more than gigantic bird chasing two perfectly insignificant butterflies among white mountains, then you can just begin to imagine the twistings, dodgings, hairbreadth escapes, and the wild zigzag rush of that flight home. More than once, before they got even half way, Roverandom's tail was singed by the dragon's breath.

What was the Man-in-the-Moon doing? Well, he let off a truly magnificent rocket; and after that he said 'Drat that creature!' and also 'Drat those puppies! They will bring on an eclipse before it is due!' And then he went down into the cellars and uncorked a dark, black spell that looked like jellified tar and honey (and smelt like the Fifth of November and cabbage boiling over).

At that very moment the dragon swooped up right above the tower and lifted a huge claw to bat Roverandom – bat him right off into the blank nowhere. But he never did. The Man-in-the-Moon shot the spell up out of a lower window, and hit the dragon splosh on the stomach (where all dragons are peculiarly tender), and knocked him crank-sideways. He lost all his wits, and flew bang into a mountain before he could get his steering right; and it was difficult to say which was most damaged, his nose or the mountain – both were out of shape.

So the two dogs fell in through the top window, and never got back their breath for a week; and the dragon slowly made his lopsided way home, where he rubbed his nose for months. The next eclipse was a failure, for the dragon was too busy licking his tummy to attend to it. And he never got the black sploshes off where the spell hit him. I am afraid they will last for ever. They call him the Mottled Monster now.

3

THE NEXT DAY the Man-in-the-Moon looked at Roverandom and said: 'That was a narrow squeak! You seem to have explored the white side pretty well for a young dog. I think, when you have got your breath back, it will be time for you to visit the other side.'

'Can I come too?' asked the moon-dog.

'It wouldn't be good for you,' said the Man, 'and I don't advise you to. You might see things that would make you more homesick than fire and chimney-stacks, and that would turn out as bad as dragons.'

The moon-dog did not blush, because he could not; and he did not say anything, but he went and sat down in a corner and wondered how much the old man knew of everything that went on, and everything that was said, too. Also for a little while he wondered what exactly the old man meant; but that did not bother him long – he was a lighthearted fellow.

As for Roverandom, when he had got his breath back, a few days later, the Man-in-the-Moon came and whistled for him. Then down and down they went together; down the stairs, and into the cellars which were cut inside the cliff and had small windows looking out of the side of the precipice over the wide places of the moon; and then down secret steps that seemed to lead right under the mountains, until after a long while they came into a completely dark place, and stopped, though Roverandom's head went on turning giddily after the miles of corkscrewing downwards.

In complete darkness the Man-in-the-Moon shone palely all by himself like a glow-worm, and that was all the light they had. It was quite enough, though, to see the door by – a big door in the floor. This the old man pulled up, and as it was lifted darkness seemed to well up out of the opening like a fog, so that Roverandom could no longer see even the faint glimmering of the Man through it.

'Down you go, good dog!' said his voice out of the blackness. And you won't be surprised to be told that Roverandom was not a good dog, and would not budge. He backed into the furthest corner of the little room, and set his ears back. He was more frightened of that hole than of the old man.

But it was not any good. The Man-in-the-Moon simply picked him up and dropped him plump into the black hole; and as he fell and fell into nothing, Roverandom heard him calling out, already far above him: 'Drop straight, and then fly on with the wind! Wait for me at the other end!'

That ought to have comforted him, but it did not. Roverandom always said afterwards that he did not think even falling over the world's edge could be worse; and that anyway it was the nastiest part of all his adventures, and still made him feel as if he had lost his tummy whenever he thought of it. You can tell he is still thinking of it when he cries out and twitches in his sleep on the hearthrug.

All the same, it came to an end. After a long while his falling gradually slowed down, until at last he almost stopped. The rest of the way he had to use his wings; and it was like flying up, up, through a big chimney – luckily with a strong draught helping him along. Jolly glad he was when he got at last to the top.

There he lay panting at the edge of the hole at the other end, waiting obediently, and anxiously, for the Man-in-the-Moon. It was a good while before he appeared, and Roverandom had time to see that he was at the bottom of a deep dark valley, ringed round with low dark hills. Black clouds seemed to rest upon their tops; and beyond the clouds was just one star.

Suddenly the little dog felt very sleepy; a bird in some gloomy bushes nearby was singing a drowsy song that seemed strange and wonderful to him after the little dumb birds of the other side to which he had got used. He shut his eyes.

'Wake up, you doglet!' called a voice; and Roverandom bounced up just in time to see the Man climbing out of the hole on a silver rope which a large grey spider (much larger than himself) was fastening to a tree close by.

The Man climbed out. 'Thank you!' he said to the spider. 'And now be off!' And off the spider went, and was glad to go. There are black spiders on the dark side, poisonous ones, if not as large as the monsters of the white side. They hate anything white or pale or light, and especially pale spiders, which they hate like rich relations that pay infrequent visits.

The grey spider dropped back down the rope into the hole, and a black spider dropped out of the tree at the same moment.

'Now then!' cried the old man to the black spider.

'Come back there! That is my private door, and don't you forget it. Just make me a nice hammock from those two yew-trees, and I'll forgive you.

'It's a longish climb down and up through the middle of the moon,' he said to Roverandom, 'and I think a little rest before they arrive would do me good. They are very nice, but they need a good deal of energy. Of course I could take to wings, only I wear 'em out so fast; also it would mean widening the hole, as my size in wings would hardly fit, and I'm a beautiful rope-climber.

'Now what do you think of this side?' the Man continued. 'Dark with a pale sky, while tother was pale with a dark sky, eh? Quite a change, only there is not much more real colour here than there, not what I call real colour, loud and lots of it together. There are a few gleams under the trees, if you look, fireflies and diamond-beetles and ruby-moths, and such like. Too tiny, though; too tiny like all the bright things on this side. And they live a terrible life of it, what with owls like eagles and as black as coal, and crows like vultures and as numerous as sparrows, and all these black spiders. It's the black-velvet bob-owlers, flying all together in clouds, that I personally like least. They won't even get out of *my* way; I hardly dare give out a glimmer, or they all get tangled in my beard.

'Still this side has its charms, young dog; and one of them is that nobody and no-doggy on earth has ever seen it before – when they were awake – except you!'

Then the Man suddenly jumped into the hammock, which the black spider had been spinning for him while he was talking, and went fast asleep in a twinkling.

Roverandom sat alone and watched him, with a wary eye for black spiders too. Little gleams of firelight, red, green, gold, and blue, flashed and shifted here and there beneath the dark windless trees. The sky was pale with strange stars above the floating wisps of velvet cloud. Thousands of nightingales seemed to be singing in some other valley, faint beyond the nearer hills. And then Roverandom heard the sound of children's voices, or the echo of the echo of their voices coming down a sudden soft-stirring breeze. He sat up and barked the loudest bark he had barked since this tale began.

'Bless me!' cried the Man-in-the-Moon, jumping up wide awake, straight out of the hammock onto the grass, and nearly onto Roverandom's tail. 'Have they arrived already?'

'Who?' asked Roverandom.

'Well, if you didn't hear them, what did you yap for?' said the old man. 'Come on! This is the way.'

They went down a long grey path, marked at the sides with faintly luminous stones, and overhung with bushes. It led on and on, and the bushes became pine-trees, and the air was filled with the smell of pine-trees at night. Then the path began to climb; and after a time they came to the top of the lowest point in the ring of hills that had shut them in.

Then Roverandom looked down into the next valley; and all the nightingales stopped singing, like turning off a tap, and children's voices floated up clear and sweet, for they were singing a fair song with many voices blended to one music.

Down the hillside raced and jumped the old man and

the dog together. My word! the Man-in-the-Moon could leap from rock to rock!

'Come on, come on!' he called. 'I may be a bearded billy-goat, a wild or garden goat, but you can't catch me!' And Roverandom had to fly to keep up with him.

And so they came suddenly to a sheer precipice, not very high, but dark and polished like jet. Looking over, Roverandom saw below a garden in twilight; and as he looked it changed to the soft glow of an afternoon sun, though he could not see where the soft light came from that lit all that sheltered place and never strayed beyond. Grey fountains were there, and long lawns; and children everywhere, dancing sleepily, walking dreamily, and talking to themselves. Some stirred as if just waking from deep sleep; some were already running wide awake and laughing: they were digging, gathering flowers, building tents and houses, chasing butterflies, kicking balls, climbing trees; and all were singing.

'Where do they all come from?' asked Roverandom, bewildered and delighted.

'From their homes and beds, of course,' said the Man.

'And how do they get here?'

'That I ain't going to tell you at all; and you'll never find out. You are lucky, and so is anyone, to get here by any way at all; but the children don't come by your way, at any rate. Some come often, and some come seldom, and I make most of the dream. Some of it they bring with them, of course, like lunch to school, and some (I am sorry to say) the spiders make – but not in this valley, and not if I catch 'em at it. And now let's go and join the party!'

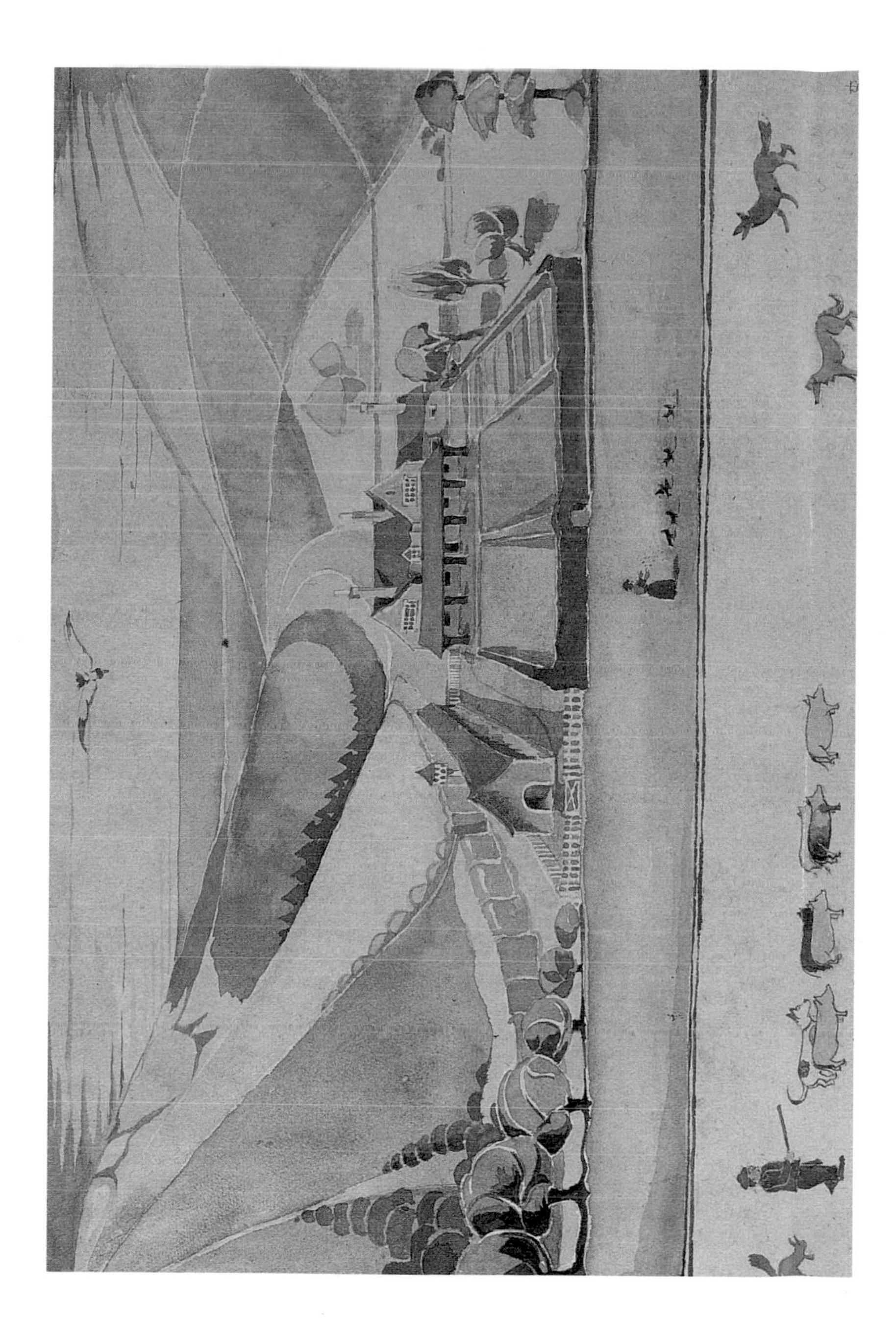

The White Dragon pursues Roverandom & the Moondog.

1925

The cliff of jet sloped steeply down. It was much too smooth even for a spider to climb – not that any spider ever dared try; for he might slide down, but neither he nor anything else could get up again; and in that garden were hidden sentinels, not to mention the Man-in-the-Moon, without whom no party was complete, for they were his own parties.

And he now slid bang into the middle of this one. He just sat down and tobogganed, swish! right into the midst of a crowd of children with Roverandom rolling on top of him, quite forgetting that he could fly. Or could have flown – for when he picked himself up at the bottom he found that his wings had gone.

'What's that little dog doing?' said a small boy to the Man. Roverandom was going round and round like a top, trying to look at his own back.

'Looking for his wings, my boy. He thinks he has rubbed them off on the toboggan-run, but they're in my pocket. No wings allowed down here, people don't get out of here without leave, do they?'

'No! Daddy-long-beard!' said about twenty children all at once, and one boy caught hold of the old man's beard and climbed up it onto his shoulder. Roverandom expected to see him turned into a moth or a piece of indiarubber, or something, on the spot.

But 'My word! you're a bit of a rope-climber, my boy!' said the Man. 'I'll have to give you lessons.' And he tossed the boy right up into the air. He did not fall down again; not a bit of it. He stuck up in the air; and the Man-in-the-Moon threw him a silver rope that he slipped out of his pocket.

'Just climb down that quick!' he said; and down the

boy slithered into the old man's arms, where he was well tickled. 'You'll wake up, if you laugh so loud,' said the Man, and he put him down on the grass and walked off into the crowd.

Roverandom was left to amuse himself, and he was just making for a beautiful yellow ball ('Just like my own at home,' he thought) when he heard a voice he knew.

'There's my little dog!' it said. 'There's my little dog! I always thought he was real. Fancy him being here, when I've looked and looked all over the sands and called and whistled every day for him!'

As soon as Roverandom heard that voice, he sat up and begged.

'My little begging dog!' said little boy Two (of course); and he ran up and patted him. 'Where have you been to?'

But all Roverandom could say at first was: 'Can you hear what I'm saying?'

'Of course I can,' said little boy Two. 'But when mummy brought you home before, you wouldn't listen to me at all, although I did my best bark-talk for you. And I don't believe you tried to say much to me either; you seemed to be thinking of something else.'

Roverandom said how sorry he was, and he told the little boy how he had fallen out of his pocket; and all about Psamathos, and Mew, and many of the adventures he had had since he was lost. That is how the little boy and his brothers got to know about the odd fellow in the sand, and learned a lot of other useful things they might otherwise have missed. Little boy Two thought that 'Roverandom' was a splendid name. 'I shall call you that too,' he said. 'And don't forget that you still belong to me!'

Then they had a game with the ball, and a game of hide-and-seek, and a run and a long walk, and a rabbit-hunt (with no result, of course, except excitement: the rabbits were exceedingly shadowy), and much splashing in the ponds, and all kinds of other things one after another for endless ages; and they got to like one another better and better. The little boy was rolling over and over on the dewy grass, in a very bed-timish light (but no one seems to mind wet grass or bed-time in that place), and the little dog was rolling over and over with him, and standing on his head like no dog on earth ever has done since Mother Hubbard's dead dog did it; and the little boy was laughing till he — vanished quite suddenly and left Roverandom all alone on the lawn!

'He's waked up, that's all,' said the Man-in-the-Moon, who suddenly appeared. 'Gone home, and about time too. Why! it's only a quarter of an hour before his breakfast time. He'll miss his walk on the sands this morning. Well, well! I am afraid it's our time to go, too.'

So, very reluctantly, Roverandom went back to the white side with the old man. They walked all the way, and it took a very long time; and Roverandom did not enjoy it as much as he ought to have done. For they saw all kinds of queer things, and had many adventures – perfectly safe, of course, with the Man-in-the-Moon close at hand. That was just as well, as there were lots of nasty creepy things in the bogs that would otherwise have grabbed the little dog quick. The dark side was as wet as the white side was dry, and full of the most extraordinary plants and creatures, which I would tell you about, if Roverandom had taken any particular notice of them. But he did not; he was thinking of the garden and the little boy.

At last they came to the grey edge, and they looked past the cinder valleys where many of the dragons lived, through a gap in the mountains to the great white plain and the shining cliffs. They saw the world rise, a pale green and gold moon, huge and round above the shoulders of the Lunar Mountains; and Roverandom thought: 'That is where my little boy lives!' It seemed a terrible and enormous way away.

'Do dreams come true?' he asked.

'Some of mine do,' said the old man. 'Some, but not all; and seldom any of them straight away, or quite like they were in dreaming them. But why do you want to know about dreams?'

'I was only wondering,' said Roverandom.

'About that little boy,' said the Man. 'I thought so.' He then pulled a telescope out of his pocket. It opened out to an enormous length. 'A little look will do you no harm, I think,' he said.

Roverandom looked through it – when he had managed at last to shut one eye and keep the other open. He saw the world plainly. First he saw the far end of the moon's path falling straight onto the sea; and he thought he saw, faint and rather thin, long lines of small people sailing swiftly down it, but he could not be quite sure. The moonlight quickly faded. Sunlight began to grow; and suddenly there was the cove of the sand-sorcerer (but no sign of Psamathos – Psamathos did not allow himself to be peeped at); and after a while the two little boys walked into the round picture, going hand in hand along the shore. 'Looking for shells or for me?' wondered the dog.

Very soon the picture shifted and he saw the little boys' father's white house on the cliff, with its garden running down to the sea; and at the gate he saw – an unpleasant surprise – the old wizard sitting on a stone smoking his pipe, as if he had nothing to do but watch there for ever, with his old green hat on the back of his head and his waistcoat unbuttoned.

'What's old Arta-what-d'you-call-him doing at the gate?' Roverandom asked. 'I should have thought he had forgotten about me long ago. And aren't his holidays over yet?'

'No, he's waiting for you, my doglet. He hasn't forgotten. If you turn up there just now, real or toy, he'll put some new bewitchment on you pretty quick. It isn't that he minds so much about his trousers – they were soon mended – but he is very annoyed with Samathos for interfering; and Samathos hasn't finished making his arrangements yet for dealing with him.'

Just then Roverandom saw Artaxerxes' hat blown off by the wind, and off the wizard ran after it; and plain to see, he had a wonderful patch on his trousers, an orange-coloured patch with black spots.

'I should have thought that a wizard could have managed to patch his trousers better than that!' said Roverandom.

'But he thinks he has managed it beautifully!' said the old man. 'He bewitched a piece off somebody's window-curtains; they got fire insurance, and he got a splash of colour, and both are satisfied. Still, you are right. He is failing, I do believe. Sad after all these centuries to see a man going off his magic; but lucky for you, perhaps.' Then the Man-in-the-Moon closed the telescope with a snap, and off they went again.

'Here are your wings again,' he said when they had reached the tower. 'Now fly off and amuse yourself! Don't worry the moonbeams, don't kill my white rabbits, and come back when you feel hungry! – or have any other sort of pain.'

Roverandom at once flew off to find the moon-dog and tell him about the other side; but the other dog was a bit jealous of a visitor being allowed to see things which he could not, and he pretended not to be interested.

'Sounds a nasty part altogether,' he growled. 'I'm sure I don't want to see it. I suppose you'll be bored with the white side now, and only having me to go about with, instead of all your two-legged friends. It's a pity the Persian wizard is such a sticker, and you can't go home.'

Roverandom was rather hurt; and he told the moon-dog over and over again that he was jolly glad to be back at the tower, and would never be bored with the white side. They soon settled down to be good friends again, and did lots and lots of things together; and yet what the moon-dog had said in bad temper turned out to be true. It was not Roverandom's fault, and he did his best not to show it, but somehow none of the adventures or explorations seemed so exciting to him as they had done before, and he was always thinking of the fun he had in the garden with little boy Two.

They visited the valley of the white moon-gnomes (moonums, for short) that ride about on rabbits, and make pancakes out of snowflakes, and grow little golden apple-trees no bigger than buttercups in their neat orchards. They put broken glass and tintacks outside the lairs of some of the lesser dragons (while they were asleep), and lay awake till the middle of the night to hear them roar with rage – dragons often have tender tummies, as I have told you already, and they go out for a drink at twelve midnight every night of their lives, not to speak of between-whiles. Sometimes the dogs even dared to go spider-baiting – biting webs and setting free the moonbeams, and flying off just in time, while the spiders threw lassoes at them from the hill-tops. But all the while Roverandom was looking out for Postman Mew and News of the World (mostly murders and football-matches, as even a little dog knows; but there is sometimes something better in an odd corner).

He missed Mew's next visit, as he was away on a ramble, but the old man was still reading the letters and news when he got back (and he seemed in a mighty good humour too, sitting on the roof with his feet dangling over the edge, puffing at an enormous white clay-pipe, sending out clouds of smoke like a railway-engine, and smiling right round his round old face).

Roverandom felt he could bear it no longer. 'I've got a pain in my inside,' he said. 'I want to go back to the little boy, so that his dream can come true.'

The old man put down his letter (it was about Artaxerxes, and very amusing), and took the pipe out of his mouth. 'Must you go? Can't you stay? This is so sudden! So pleased to have met you! You must drop in again one day. *Dee*lighted to see you any time!' he said all in a breath.

'Very well!' he went on more sensibly. 'Artaxerxes is arranged for.'

'How??' asked Roverandom, really excited again.

'He has married a mermaid and gone to live at the bottom of the Deep Blue Sea.'

'I hope she will patch his trousers better! A green seaweed patch would go well with his green hat.'

'My dear dog! He was married in a complete new suit of seaweed green with pink coral buttons and epaulettes of sea-anemones; and they burnt his old hat on the beach! Samathos arranged it all. O! Samathos is very deep, as deep as the Deep Blue Sea, and I expect he means to settle lots of things to his liking this way, lots more than just you, my dog.

'I wonder how it will turn out! Artaxerxes is getting into his twentieth or twenty-first childhood at the moment, it seems to me; and he makes a lot of fuss about very little things. Most obstinate he is, to be sure. He used to be a pretty good magician, but he is becoming bad-tempered and a thorough nuisance. When he came and dug up old Samathos with a wooden spade in the middle of the afternoon, and pulled him out of his hole by the ears, the Samathist thought things had gone too far, and I don't wonder. "Such a lot of disturbance, just at my best time for sleeping, and all about a wretched little dog": that is what he writes to me, and you needn't blush.

'So he invited Artaxerxes to a mermaid-party, when

both their tempers had cooled down a bit, and that is how it all happened. They took Artaxerxes out for a moonlight swim, and he will never go back to Persia, or even Pershore. He fell in love with the rich mer-king's elderly but lovely daughter, and they were married the next night.

'It is probably just as well. There has not been a resident Magician in the Ocean for some time. Proteus, Poseidon, Triton, Neptune, and all that lot, they've all turned into minnows or mussels long ago, and in any case they never knew or bothered much about things outside the Mediterranean – they were too fond of sardines. Old Niord retired a long while ago, too. He was of course only able to give half his attention to business after his silly marriage with the giantess – you remember she fell in love with him because he had clean feet (so convenient in the home), and fell out of love with him, when it was too late, because they were wet. He's on his last legs now, I hear; quite doddery, poor old dear. Oil-fuel has given him a dreadful cough, and he has retired to the coast of Iceland for a little sunshine.

'There was the Old Man of the Sea, of course. He was my cousin, and I'm not proud of it. He was a bit of a burden – wouldn't walk, and always wanted to be carried, as I dare say you have heard. That was the death of him. He sat on a floating mine (if you know what I mean) a year or two ago, right on one of the buttons! Not even *my* magic could do anything with that case. It was worse than the one of Humpty Dumpty.'

'What about Britannia?' asked Roverandom, who after all was an English dog; though really he was a bit bored with all this, and wanted to hear more about his own wizard. 'I thought Britannia ruled the waves.'

'She never really gets her feet wet. She prefers patting lions on the beach, and sitting on a penny with an eel-fork in her hand – and in any case there is more to manage in the sea than waves. Now they have got Artaxerxes, and I hope he will be of use. He'll spend the first few years trying to grow plums on polyps, I expect, if they let him; and that'll be easier than keeping the mer-folk in order.

'Well, well, well! Where was I? Of course – you can go back now, if you want to. In fact, not to be too polite, it's time you went back as soon as possible. Old Samathos is your first call – and don't follow my bad example and forget your Ps when you meet!'

Mew turned up again the very next day, with an extra post – an immense number of letters for the Man-in-the-Moon, and bundles of newspapers: *The Illustrated Weekly Weed*, *Ocean Notions*, *The Mer-mail*, *The Conch*, and *The Morning Splash*. They all had exactly the same (exclusive) pictures of Artaxerxes' wedding on the beach at full moon, with Mr Psamathos Psamathides, the well-known financier (a mere title of respect), grinning in the background. But they were nicer than our pictures, for they were at least coloured; and the mermaid really did look beautiful (her tail was in the foam).

The time had come to say good-bye. The Man-in-the-Moon beamed on Roverandom; and the moon-dog tried to look unconcerned. Roverandom himself had rather a drooping tail, but all he said was: 'Good-bye, pup! Take care of yourself, don't worry the moon-beams, don't kill the white rabbits, and don't eat too much supper!'

'Pup yourself!' said the moon-Rover. 'And stop eating wizards' trousers!' That was all; and yet, I believe, he was always worrying the old Man-in-the-Moon to send him on a holiday to visit Roverandom, and that he has been allowed to go several times since then.

After that Roverandom went back with Mew, and the Man went back into his cellars, and the moon-dog sat on the roof and watched them out of sight.

4

THERE WAS A COLD WIND blowing off the North Star when they got near the world's edge, and the chilly spray of the waterfalls splashed over them. It had been stiffer going on the way back, for old Psamathos' magic was not in such a hurry just then; and they were glad to rest on the Isle of Dogs. But as Roverandom was still his enchanted size, he did not enjoy himself much there. The other dogs were too large and noisy, and too scornful; and the bones of the bone-trees were too large and bony.

It was dawn of the day after the day after tomorrow when at last they sighted the black cliffs of Mew's home; and the sun was warm on their backs, and the tips of the sand-hillocks were already pale and dry, by the time they alighted in the cove of Psamathos.

Mew gave a little cry, and tapped with his beak on a bit of wood lying on the ground. The bit of wood immediately grew straight up into the air, and turned into Psamathos' left ear, and was joined by another ear, and quickly followed by the rest of the sorcerer's ugly head and neck.

'What do you two want at this time of day?' growled Psamathos. 'It's my favourite time for sleep.'

'We're back!' said the seagull.

'And you've allowed yourself to be carried back on his back, I see,' Psamathos said, turning to the little dog.

'After dragon-hunting I should have thought you would have found a little flight back home quite easy.'

'But please, sir,' said Roverandom, 'I left my wings behind; they didn't really belong to me. And I should rather like to be an ordinary dog again.'

'O! all right. Still I hope you have enjoyed yourself as "Roverandom". You ought to have done. Now you can be just Rover again, if you really want to be; and you can go home and play with your yellow ball, and sleep on armchairs when you get the chance, and sit on laps, and be a respectable little yap-dog again.'

'What about the little boy?' said Rover.

'But you ran away from him, silly, all the way to the moon, I thought!' said Psamathos, pretending to be annoyed and surprised, but giving a merry twinkle out of one knowing eye. 'Home I said, and home I meant. Don't splutter and argue!'

Poor Rover was spluttering because he was trying to get in a very polite 'Mr P-samathos'. Eventually he did.

'P-P-Please, Mr P-P-P-samathos,' he said, most touchingly. 'P-Please p-pardon me, but I have met him again; and I shouldn't run away now; and really I belong to him, don't I? So I ought to go back to him.'

'Stuff and nonsense! Of course you don't and oughtn't! You belong to the old lady that bought you first, and back you'll have to go to her. You can't buy stolen goods, or bewitched ones either, as you would know, if you knew the Law, you silly little dog. Little boy Two's mother wasted sixpence on you, and that's an end of it. And what's in dream-meetings anyway?' wound up Psamathos with a huge wink.

'I thought some of the Man-in-the-Moon's dreams came true,' said little Rover sadly.

'O! did you! Well that's the Man-in-the-Moon's affair. *My* business is to change you back at once into your proper size, and send you back where you belong. Artaxerxes has departed to other spheres of usefulness, so we needn't bother about him any more. Come here!'

He took hold of Rover, and he waved his fat hand over the little dog's head, and hey presto — there was no change at all! He did it all over again, and still there was no change.

Then Psamathos got right up out of the sand, and Rover saw for the first time that he had legs like a rabbit. He stamped and ramped, and kicked sand into the air, and trampled on the seashells, and snorted like an angry pug-dog; and still nothing happened at all!

'Done by a seaweed wizard, blister and wart him!' he swore. 'Done by a Persian plum-picker, pot and jam him!' he shouted, and kept on shouting till he was tired. Then he sat down.

'Well, well!' he said at last when he was cooler. 'Live and learn! But Artaxerxes is most peculiar. Who could have guessed that he would remember you amidst all the excitement of his wedding, and go and waste his strongest incantation on a dog before going on his honeymoon – as if his first spell wasn't more than any silly little puppy is worth? If it isn't enough to split one's skin.

'Well! I don't need to think out what is to be done, at any rate,' Psamathos continued. 'There is only one possible thing. You have got to go and find him and beg his pardon. But my word! I'll remember this against him, till the sea is twice as salt and half as wet. Just you two go for a walk, and be back in half an hour when my temper's better!'

Mew and Rover went along the shore and up the cliff, Mew flying slowly and Rover trotting along very sad. They stopped outside the little boys' father's house; and Rover even went in at the gate, and sat in a flower-bed under the boys' window. It was still very early, but he barked and barked hopefully. The little boys were either still fast asleep or away, for nobody came to the window. Or so Rover thought. He had forgotten that things are different on the world from the back-garden of the moon, and that Artaxerxes' bewitchment was still on his size, and the size of his bark.

After a little while Mew took him mournfully back to the cove. There an altogether new surprise was waiting for him. Psamathos was talking to a whale! A very large whale, Uin the oldest of the Right Whales. He looked like a mountain to little Rover, lying with his great head in a deep pool near the water's edge.

'Sorry I couldn't get anything smaller at a moment's notice,' said Psamathos. 'But he is very comfortable!'

'Walk in!' said the whale.

'Good-bye! Walk in!' said the seagull.

'Walk in!' said Psamathos; 'and be quick about it! And don't bite or scratch about inside; you might give Uin a cough, and that you would find uncomfy.'

This was almost as bad as being asked to jump into the hole in the Man-in-the-Moon's cellar, and Rover backed away, so that Mew and Psamathos had to push him in. Push him they did, too, without a coax; and the whale's jaws shut to with a snap.

Inside it was very dark indeed, and fishy. There Rover sat and trembled; and as he sat (not daring even to scratch his own ears) he heard, or thought he heard, the swish and beating of the whale's tail in the waters; and he felt, or thought he felt, the whale plunge deeper and downer towards the bottom of the Deep Blue Sea.

But when the whale stopped and opened his mouth wide again (delighted to do so: whales prefer going about trawling with their jaws wide open and a good tide of food coming in, but Uin was a considerate animal) and Rover peeped out, it was deep, altogether immeasurably deep, but not at all blue. There was only a pale green light; and Rover walked out to find himself on a white path of sand winding through a dim and fantastic forest.

'Straight along! You haven't far to go,' said Uin.

Rover went straight along, as straight as the path would allow, and soon before him he saw the gate of a great palace, made it seemed of pink and white stone that shone with a pale light coming through it; and through the many windows lights of green and blue shone clear. All round the walls huge sea-trees grew, taller than the domes of the palace that swelled up vast, gleaming in the dark water. The great indiarubber trunks of the trees bent and swayed like grasses, and the shadow of their endless branches was thronged with goldfish, and silverfish, and redfish, and bluefish, and phosphorescent fish like birds. But the fishes did not sing. The mermaids sang inside the palace. How they sang! And all the sea-fairies sang in chorus, and the music floated out of the windows, hundreds of mer-folk playing on horns and pipes and conches of shell.

Sea-goblins were grinning at him out of the darkness under the trees, and Rover hurried along as fast as he could – he found his steps slow and laden deep down under the water. And why didn't he drown? I don't know, but I suppose Psamathos Psamathides had given some thought to it (he knows much more about the sea than most people would think, even though he never sets toe in it, if he can help it), while Rover and Mew had gone for a walk, and he had sat and simmered down and thought of a new plan.

Anyway Rover did not drown; but he was already wishing he was somewhere else, even in the whale's wet inside, before he got to the door: such queer shapes and faces peered at him out of the purple bushes and the spongey thickets beside the path that he felt very unsafe indeed. At last he got to the enormous door – a golden archway fringed with coral, and a door of mother-of-pearl studded with sharks' teeth. The knocker was a huge ring encrusted with white barnacles, and all the barnacles' little red streamers were hanging out; but of course Rover could not reach it, nor could he have moved it anyway. So he barked, and to his surprise his bark came quite loud. The music inside stopped at the third bark, and the door opened.

Who do you think opened it? Artaxerxes himself, dressed in what looked like plum-coloured velvet, and green silk trousers; and he still had a large pipe in his mouth, only it was blowing beautiful rainbow-coloured bubbles instead of tobacco-smoke; but he had no hat.

'Hullo!' he said. 'So you've turned up! I thought you would get tired of old P-samathos' (how he snorted over that exaggerated *P*) 'before long. He can't do quite everything. Well, what have you come down here for? We are just having a party, and you're interrupting the music.'

'Please, Mr Artcrxaxes, I mean Ertaxarxes,' began Rover, rather flustered and trying to be very polite.

'O never mind about getting it right! I don't mind!' said the wizard rather crossly. 'Get on to the explanation, and make it short; I've no time for long rigmaroles.' He had become rather full of his own importance (with strangers), since his marriage to the rich merking's daughter, and his appointment to the post of Pacific and Atlantic Magician (the PAM they called him for short, when he was not present). 'If you want to see me about anything pressing, you had better come in and wait in the hall; I might find a moment after the dance.'

He closed the door behind Rover and went off. The little dog found himself in a huge dark space under a dimly-lighted dome. There were pointed archways curtained with seaweed all round, and most of them were dark; but one of them was full of light, and music came loudly through it, music that seemed to go on and on for ever, never repeating and never stopping for a rest.

Rover soon got very tired of waiting, so he walked along to the shining doorway and peeped through the curtains. He was looking into a vast ballroom with seven domes and ten thousand coral pillars, lit with purest magic and filled with warm and sparkling water. There all the golden-haired mermaids and the dark-haired sirens were dancing interwoven dances as they sang – not dancing on their tails, but wonderful swim-dancing, up and down, as well as to and fro, in the clear water.

Nobody noticed the little dog's nose peeping through the seaweed at the door, so after gazing for a while he crept inside. The floor was made of silver sand and pink butterfly shells, all open and flapping in the gently swirling water, and he had picked his way carefully among them for some way, keeping close to the wall, before a voice said suddenly above him:

'What a sweet little dog! He's a land-dog, not a sea-dog, I'm sure. How could he have got here – such a tiny mite!'

Rover looked up and saw a beautiful mer-lady with a large black comb in her golden hair, sitting on a ledge not far above him; her regrettable tail was dangling down, and she was mending one of Artaxerxes' green socks. She was, of course, the new Mrs Artaxerxes (usually known as Princess Pam; she was rather popular, which was more than you could say for her husband). Artaxerxes was at the moment sitting beside her, and whether he had the time or not for long rigmaroles, he was listening to one of his wife's. Or had been, before Rover turned up. Mrs Artaxerxes put an end to her rigmarole, and to her sock-mending, as soon as she caught sight of him, and floating down picked him up and carried him back to her couch. This was really a window-seat on the first floor (an indoors window) – there are no stairs in sea-houses, and no umbrellas, and for the same reason; and there is not much difference between doors and windows, either.

The mer-lady soon settled her beautiful (and rather capacious) self comfortably on her couch again, and put Rover on her lap; and immediately there was an awful growl from under the window-seat.

'Lie down, Rover! Lie down, good dog!' said Mrs Artaxerxes. She was not talking to our Rover, though; she was talking to a white mer-dog who came out now, in spite of what she said, growling and grumbling and beating the water with his little web-feet, and lashing it with his large flat tail, and blowing bubbles out of his sharp nose.

'What a horrible little thing!' the new dog said. 'Look at his miserable tail! Look at his feet! Look at his silly coat!'

'Look at yourself,' said Rover from the mer-lady's lap, 'and you won't want to do it again! Who called you Rover? – a cross between a duck and a tadpole pretending to be a dog!' From which you can see that they took rather a fancy to one another at first sight.

Indeed, they soon made great friends – not quite such friends, perhaps, as Rover and the moon-dog, if only because Rover's stay under the sea was shorter, and the deeps are not such a jolly place as the moon for little dogs, being full of dark and awful places where light has never been and never will be, because they will never be uncovered till light has all gone out. Horrible things live there, too old for imagining, too strong for spells, too vast for measurement. Artaxerxes had already found that out. The post of PAM is not the most comfortable job in the world.

'Now swim away and amuse yourselves!' said his wife, when the dog-argument had died down and the two animals were merely sniffing at one another. 'Don't worry the fire-fish, don't chew the sea-anemones, don't get caught in the clams; and come back to supper!'

'Please, I can't swim,' said Rover.

'Dear me! What a nuisance!' she said. 'Now Pam!' – she was the only one so far that called him this to his face – 'here is something you can really do, at last!'

'Certainly, my dear!' said the wizard, very anxious to oblige her, and pleased to be able to show that he really had some magic, and was not an entirely useless official (limpets they call them in sea-language). He took a little wand out of his waistcoat-pocket – it was really his fountain-pen, but it was no longer any use for writing: mer-folk use a queer sticky ink that is absolutely no use in fountain-pens – and he waved it over Rover.

Artaxerxes was, in spite of what some people have said, a very good magician in his own way (or Rover would never have had these adventures) – rather a minor art, but still needing a deal of practice. Anyway after the very first wave Rover's tail began to get fishy and his feet to get webby, and his coat to get more and more like a mackintosh. When the change was over, he soon got used to it; and he found swimming a good deal easier to pick up than flying, very nearly as pleasant, and not so tiring – unless you wanted to go down.

The first thing he did, after a trial swim round the ballroom, was to bite at the other dog's tail. In fun, of course; but fun or not, there was nearly a fight on the spot, for the mer-dog was a bit touchy-tempered. Rover only saved himself by making off as fast as possible; nimble and quick he had to be, too. My word! there was a chase, in and out of windows, and along dark passages, and round pillars, and out and up and round the domes; till at last the mer-dog himself was exhausted, and his bad temper too, and they sat down together on the top of the highest cupola next to the flag-pole. The mer-king's banner, a seaweed streamer of scarlet and green, spangled with pearls, was floating from it.

'What's your name?' said the mer-dog after a breathless pause. 'Rover?' he said. 'That's my name, so you can't have it. I had it first!'

'How do you know?'

'Of course I know! I can see you are only a puppy, and you have not been down here hardly five minutes. I was enchanted ages and ages ago, hundreds of years. I expect I'm the first of all the dog Rovers.

'My first master was a Rover, a real one, a sea-rover who sailed his ship in the northern waters; it was a long ship with red sails, and it was carved like a dragon at the prow, and he called it the Red Worm and loved it. I loved him, though I was only a puppy, and he did not notice me much; for I wasn't big enough to go hunting, and he didn't take dogs to sail with him. One day I went sailing without being asked. He was saying farewell to his wife; the wind was blowing, and the men were thrusting the Red Worm out over the rollers into the sea. The foam was white about the dragon's neck; and I suddenly felt that I should not see him again after that day, if I didn't go too. I sneaked on board somehow, and hid behind a water-barrel; and we were far at sea and the landmarks low in the water before they found me.

'That's when they called me Rover, when they dragged me out by my tail. "Here's a fine sea-rover!" said one. "And a strange fate is on him, that turns never home," said another with queer eyes. And indeed

I never did go back home; and I have never grown any bigger, though I have grown much older – and wiser, of course.

'There was a sea-fight on that voyage, and I ran up on the fore-deck while the arrows fell and sword clashed upon shield. But the men of the Black Swan boarded us, and drove my master's men all over the side. He was the last to go. He stood beside the dragon's head, and then he dived into the sea in all his mail; and I dived after him.

'He went to the bottom quicker than I did, and the mermaids caught him; but I told them to carry him swift to land, for many would weep, if he did not come home. They smiled at me, and lifted him up, and bore him away; and now some say they carried him to the shore, and some shake their heads at me. You can't depend on mermaids, except for keeping their own secrets; they're better than oysters at that.

'I often think they really buried him in the white sand. Far away from here there lies still a part of the Red Worm that the men of the Black Swan sank; or it was there when last I passed. A forest of weed was growing round it and over it, all except the dragon's head; somehow not even barnacles were growing on that, and under it there was a mound of white sand.

'I left those parts long ago. I turned slowly into a sea-dog – the older sea-women used to do a good deal of witchcraft in those days, and one of them was kind to me. It was she that gave me as a present to the mer-king, the reigning one's grandfather, and I have been in and about the palace ever since. That's all about me. It happened hundreds of years ago, and I have seen a good deal of the high seas and the low seas since then, but I have never been back home. Now tell me about you! I suppose you don't come from the North Sea by any chance, do you? – we used to call it England's Sea in those days – or know any of the old places in and about the Orkneys?'

Our Rover had to confess that he had never heard before of anything but just 'the sea', and not much of that. 'But I have been to the moon,' he said, and he told his new friend as much about it as he could make him understand.

The mer-dog enjoyed Rover's tale immensely, and believed at least half of it. 'A jolly good yarn,' he said, 'and the best I have heard for a long time. I have seen the moon. I go on top occasionally, you know, but I never imagined it was like that. But my word! that sky-pup has got a cheek. Three Rovers! Two's bad enough, but three's impossible! And I don't believe for a moment he is older than I am; if he is a hundred yet, I should be mighty surprised.'

He was probably quite right too. The moon-dog, as you noticed, exaggerated a lot. 'And anyway,' went on the mer-dog, 'he only gave himself the name. Mine was given me.'

'And so was mine,' said our little dog.

'And for no reason at all, and before you had begun to earn it any way. I like the Man-in-the-Moon's idea. I shall call you Roverandom, too; and if I were you I should stick to it – you never do seem to know where you are going next! Let's go down to supper!'

It was a fishy supper, but Roverandom soon got used to that; it seemed to suit his webby feet. After supper he suddenly remembered why he had come all the way to the bottom of the sea; and off he went to look for Artaxerxes. He found him blowing bubbles, and turning them into real balls to please the little mer-children.

'Please, Mr Artaxerxes, could you be bothered to turn me – ' began Roverandom.

'O! go away!' said the wizard. 'Can't you see I can't be bothered? Not now, I'm busy.' This is what Artaxerxes said all too often to people he did not think were important. He knew well enough what Rover wanted; but he was not in a hurry himself.

So Roverandom swam off and went to bed, or rather roosted in a bunch of seaweed growing on a high rock in the garden. There was the old whale resting just underneath; and if anyone tells you that whales don't go down to the bottom or stop there dozing for hours, you need not let that bother you. Old Uin was in every way exceptional.

'Well?' he said. 'How have you got on? I see you are still toy-size. What's the matter with Artaxerxes? Can't he do anything, or won't he?'

'I think he can,' said Roverandom. 'Look at my new shape! But if ever I try to get onto the matter of size, he keeps on saying how busy he is, and he hasn't time for long explanations.'

'Umph!' said the whale, and knocked a tree sideways with his tail – the swish of it nearly washed Roverandom off his rock. 'I don't think that PAM will be a success in these parts; but I shouldn't worry. You'll be all right sooner or later. In the meanwhile there are lots of new things to see tomorrow. Go to sleep! Good-bye!' And he swam off into the dark. The report that he took back to the cove made old Psamathos very angry all the same.

The lights of the palace were all turned off. No moon or star came down through that deep dark water. The green got gloomier and gloomier, until it was all black, and there was not a glimmer, except when big luminous fish went by slowly through the weeds. Yet Roverandom slept soundly that night, and the next night, and several nights after. And the next day, and the day after, he looked for the wizard and couldn't find him anywhere.

One morning when he was beginning already to feel quite a sea-dog and to wonder if he had come to stay there for ever, the mer-dog said to him: 'Bother that wizard! Or rather, don't bother him! Give him a miss today. Let's go off for a really long swim!'

Off they went, and the long swim turned into an excursion lasting for days. They covered a terrific distance in the time; they were enchanted creatures, you must remember, and there were few ordinary things in the seas that could keep up with them. When they got tired of the cliffs and mountains at the bottom, and of the racing runs in the middle heights, they rose up and up and up, right through the water for a mile and a bit; and when they got to the top, no land was to be seen.

The sea all round them was smooth and calm and grey. Then it suddenly ruffled and went dark in patches under a little cold wind, the wind at dawn. Swiftly the sun looked up with a shout over the rim of the sea, red as if he had been drinking hot wine; and swiftly he leaped into the air and went off for his daily journey, turning all the edges of the waves golden and the shadows between them dark green. A ship was sailing on the margin of the sea and the sky, and it sailed right into the sun, so that its masts were black against the fire.

'Where's that going to?' asked Roverandom.

'O! Japan or Honolulu or Manila or Easter Island or Thursday or Vladivostok, or somewhere or other, I suppose,' said the mer-dog, whose geography was a bit vague, in spite of his hundreds of years of boasted prowlings. 'This is the Pacific, I believe; but I don't know which part – a warm part, by the feel of it. It's rather a large piece of water. Let's go and look for something to eat!'

When they got back, some days later, Roverandom at once went to look for the wizard again; he felt he had given him a good long rest.

'Please, Mr Artaxerxes, could you bother – ' he began as usual.

'No! I could not!' said Artaxerxes, even more definitely than usual. This time he really was busy, though. The Complaints had come in by post. Of course, as you can imagine, all kinds of things go wrong in the sea, that not even the best PAM in the ocean could prevent, and some of which he is not even supposed to have anything to do with. Wrecks come down plump now and again on the roof of somebody's sea-house; explosions occur in the sea-bed (O yes! they have volcanoes and all that kind of nuisance quite as badly as we have) and blow up somebody's prize flock of goldfish, or prize bed of anemones, or one and only pearl-oyster, or famous rock and coral garden; or savage fish have a fight in the highway and knock mer-children over; or absent-minded sharks swim in at the dining-room window and spoil the dinner; or the deep, dark, unmentionable monsters of the black abysses do horrible and wicked things.

The mer-folk have always put up with all this, but not without complaining. They liked complaining. They used of course to write letters to *The Weekly Weed*, *The Mer-mail*, and *Ocean Notions*; but they had a PAM now, and they wrote to him as well, and blamed him for *everything*, even if they got their tails nipped by their own pet lobsters. They said his magic was inadequate (as it sometimes was) and that his salary ought to be reduced (which was true but rude); and that he was too big for his boots (which was also near the mark: they should have said slippers, he was too lazy to wear boots often); and they said lots besides to worry Artaxerxes every morning, and especially on Mondays. It was always worst (by several hundred envelopes) on Mondays; and this was a Monday, so Artaxerxes threw a lump of rock at Roverandom, and he slipped off like a shrimp from a net.

He was jolly glad when he got out into the garden to find that he was still unchanged in shape; and I dare say if he had not removed himself quick the wizard would have changed him into a sea-slug, or sent him to the Back of Beyond (wherever that is), or even to Pot (which is at the bottom of the deepest sea). He was very annoyed, and he went and grumbled to the sea-Rover.

'You'd better give him a rest till Monday is over, at

any rate,' advised the mer-dog; 'and I should miss out Mondays altogether, in future, if I were you. Come and have another swim!'

After that Roverandom gave the wizard such a long rest that they almost forgot about one another – not quite: dogs don't forget lumps of rock very quickly. But to all appearances Roverandom had settled down to become a permanent pet of the palace. He was always off somewhere with the mer-dog, and often the mer-children came along as well. They were not as jolly as real, two-legged children in Roverandom's opinion (but then of course Roverandom did not really belong to the sea, and was not a perfect judge), but they kept him happy; and they might have kept him there for ever and have made him forget little boy Two in the end, if it had not been for things that happened later. You can make up your mind whether Psamathos had anything to do with these events, when we come to them.

There were plenty of these children to choose from, at any rate. The old mer-king had hundreds of daughters and thousands of grandchildren, and all in the same palace; and they were all fond of the two Rovers, and so was Mrs Artaxerxes. It was a pity that Roverandom never thought of telling her his story; she knew how to manage the PAM in any mood. But in that case, of course, Roverandom would have gone back sooner and missed many of the sights. It was with Mrs Artaxerxes, and some of the mer-children that he visited the Great White Caves, where all the jewels that are lost in the sea, and many that have always been in the sea, and of course pearls upon pearls, are hoarded and hidden.

They went too, another time, to visit the smaller sea-fairies in their little glass houses at the bottom of the sea. The sea-fairies seldom swim, but wander singing over the bed of the sea in smooth places, or drive in shell-carriages harnessed to the tiniest fishes; or else they ride astride little green crabs with bridles of fine threads (which of course don't prevent the crabs from going sideways, as they always will); and they have troubles with the sea-goblins that are larger, and ugly and rowdy, and do nothing except fight and hunt fish and gallop about on sea-horses. Those goblins can live out of the water for a long while, and play in the surf at the water's edge in a storm. So can some of the sea-fairies, but they prefer the calm warm nights of summer evenings on lonely shores (and naturally are very seldom seen in consequence).

Another day old Uin turned up again and gave the two dogs a ride for a change; it was like riding on a moving mountain. They were away for days and days; and they only turned back from the eastern edge of the world just in time. There the whale rose to the top and blew out a fountain of water so high that a lot of it was thrown right off the world and over the edge.

Another time he took them to the other side (or as near as he dared), and that was a still longer and more exciting journey, the most marvellous of all Roverandom's travels, as he realised later, when he was grown to be an older and a wiser dog. It would take the whole of another story, at least, to tell you of all their adventures in Uncharted Waters and of their glimpses of lands unknown to geography, before they passed the Shadowy Seas and reached the great Bay of Fairyland (as we call it) beyond the Magic Isles; and saw far off in the last West the Mountains of Elvenhome and the light of Faery upon the waves. Roverandom thought he caught a glimpse of the city of the Elves on the green hill beneath the Mountains, a glint of white far away; but Uin dived again so suddenly that he could not be sure. If he was right, he is one of the very few creatures, on two legs or four, who can walk about our own lands and say they have glimpsed that other land, however far away.

'I should catch it, if this was found out!' said Uin. 'No one from the Outer Lands is supposed ever to come here; and few ever do now. Mum's the word!'

What did I say about dogs? They don't forget ill-tempered lumps of rock. Well then, in spite of all these varied sight-seeings and these astonishing journeys, Roverandom kept it in his underneath mind all the time. And it came back into his upper mind, as soon as ever he got back home.

His very first thought was: 'Where's that old wizard? What's the use of being polite to him! I'll spoil his trousers again, if I get half a chance.'

He was in that frame of mind when, after trying in vain to have a word alone with Artaxerxes, he saw the magician go by, down one of the royal roads leading from the palace. He was of course too proud at his age to grow a tail or fins or learn to swim properly. The only thing he did like a fish was to drink (even in the sea, so he must have been thirsty); he spent a lot of time that might have been employed on official business conjuring up cider into large barrels in his private apartments. When he wanted to get about quickly, he drove. When Roverandom saw him, he was driving in his express – a gigantic shell shaped like a cockle and drawn by seven sharks. People got out of the way quick, for the sharks could bite.

'Let's follow!' said Roverandom to the mer-dog; and follow they did; and the two bad dogs dropped pieces of rock into the carriage whenever it passed under cliffs. They could nip along amazingly fast, as I told you; and they whizzed ahead, hid in weed-bushes and pushed anything loose they could find over the edge. It annoyed the wizard intensely, but they took care that he did not spot them.

Artaxerxes was in a very bad temper before he started, and he was in a rage before he had gone far, a rage not unmixed with anxiety. For he was going to investigate the damage done by an unusual whirlpool that had suddenly appeared – and in a part of the sea that he did not like at all; he thought (and he was quite right) that there were nasty things in that direction that were best left alone. I dare say you can guess what was the matter; Artaxerxes did. The ancient Sea-serpent was waking, or half thinking about it.

He had been in a sound sleep for years, but now he was turning. When he was uncoiled he would certainly have reached a hundred miles (some people say he would reach from Edge to Edge, but that is an exaggeration); and when he is curled up there is only one cave other than Pot (where he used to live, and many people wish him back there), only one cave in all the oceans that will hold him, and that is very unfortunately not a hundred miles from the mer-king's palace.

When he undid a curl or two in his sleep, the water heaved and shook and bent people's houses and spoilt their repose for miles and miles around. But it was very stupid to send the PAM to look into it; for of course the Sea-serpent is much too enormous and strong and old and idiotic for any one to control (primordial, prehistoric, autothalassic, fabulous, mythical, and silly are other adjectives applied to him); and Artaxerxes knew it all only too well.

Not even the Man-in-the-Moon working hard for fifty years could have concocted a spell large enough or long enough or strong enough to bind him. Only once had the Man-in-the-Moon tried (when specially requested), and at least one continent fell into the sea as a result.

Poor old Artaxerxes drove straight up to the mouth of the Sea-serpent's cave. But he had no sooner got out of his carriage than he saw the tip of the Sea-serpent's tail sticking out of the entrance; larger it was than a row of gigantic water-barrels, and green and slimy. That was quite enough for him. He wanted to go home at once before the Worm turned again – as all worms will at odd and unexpected moments.

It was little Roverandom that upset everything! He did not know anything about the Sea-serpent or its tremendousness; all he thought about was baiting the ill-tempered wizard. So when a chance came – Artaxerxes was standing staring stupid-like at the visible end of the serpent, and his steeds were taking no particular notice of anything – he crept up and bit one of the sharks' tails, for fun. For fun! What fun! The shark jumped straight forward, and the carriage jumped forward too; and Artaxerxes, who had just turned round to get into it, fell on his back. Then the shark bit the only thing it could reach at the moment, which was the shark in front; and that shark bit the next one; and so on, until the last of the seven, seeing nothing else to bite – bless me! the idiot, if he did not go and bite the Sea-serpent's tail!

The Sea-serpent gave a new and very unexpected turn! And the next thing the dogs knew was being whirled all over the place in water gone mad, bumping into giddy fishes and spinning sea-trees, scared out of their lives in a cloud of uprooted weeds, sand, shells, slugs, periwinkles, and oddments. And things got worse and worse, and the serpent kept on turning. And there was old Artaxerxes, clinging on to the reins of the sharks, being whirled all over the place too, and saying the most dreadful things to them. To the sharks, I mean. Luckily for this story, he never knew what Roverandom had done.

I don't know how the dogs got home. It was a long, long time before they did, at any rate. First of all they were washed up on the shore in one of the terrible tides caused by the Sea-serpent's stirrings; and then they were caught by fishermen on the other side of the sea and jolly nearly sent to an Aquarium (a disgusting fate); and then having escaped that by the skin of their feet they had to get all the way back themselves as best they could through perpetual subterranean commotion.

And when at last they got home there was a terrible commotion there too. All the mer-folk were crowded round the palace, all shouting at once:

'Bring out the PAM!' (Yes! they called him that publicly, and nothing longer or more dignified.) 'BRING OUT THE PAM! BRING OUT THE PAM!'

And the PAM was hiding in the cellars. Mrs Artaxerxes found him there at last, and made him come out; and all the mer-folk shouted, when he looked out of an attic-window:

'Stop this nonsense! STOP THIS NONSENSE! STOP THIS NONSENSE!'

And they made such a hullabaloo that people at all the seasides all over the world thought the sea was roaring louder than usual. It was! And all the while the Sea-serpent kept on turning, trying absentmindedly to get the tip of his tail in his mouth. But thank heavens! he was not properly and fully awake, or he might have come out and shaken his tail in anger, and then another continent would have been drowned. (Of course whether that would have been really regrettable or not depends on which continent was taken and which you live on.)

But the mer-folk did not live on a continent, but in the sea, and right in the thick of it; and very thick it was getting. And they insisted that it was the mer-king's business to make the PAM produce some spell, remedy, or solution to keep the Sea-serpent quiet: they could not get their hands to their faces to feed themselves or blow their noses, the water shook so; and everybody was bumping into everybody else; and all the fish were sea-sick, the water was so wobbly; and it was so turbid and so full of sand that everyone had coughs; and all the dancing was stopped.

Artaxerxes groaned, but he had to do something. So he went to his workshop and shut himself up for a fortnight, during which time there were three earthquakes, two submarine hurricanes, and several riots of the mer-people. Then he came out and let loose a most prodigious spell (accompanied with soothing incantation) at a distance from the cave; and everybody went home and sat in cellars waiting – everybody except Mrs Artaxerxes and her unfortunate husband. The wizard was obliged to stay (at a distance, but not a safe one) and watch the result; and Mrs Artaxerxes was obliged to stay and watch the wizard.

All the spell did was to give the Serpent a terrible bad dream: he dreamed that he was covered all over with barnacles (very irritating, and partly true), and also being slowly roasted in a volcano (very painful, and unfortunately quite imaginary). And that woke him!

Probably Artaxerxes' magic was better than was supposed. At any rate, the Sea-serpent did not come out – luckily for this story. He put his head where his tail was, and yawned, opened his mouth as wide as the cave, and snorted so loud that everyone in the cellars heard him in all the kingdoms of the sea.

And the Sea-serpent said: 'Stop this NONSENSE!'

And he added: 'If this blithering wizard doesn't go away at once, and if he ever so much as paddles in the sea again, I shall COME OUT; and I shall eat him first, and then I shall knock everything to dripping smithereens. That's all. Good night!'

And Mrs Artaxerxes carried the PAM home in a fainting fit.

When he had recovered – and that was quick, they

saw to that – he took the spell off the Serpent, and packed his bag; and all the people said and shouted:

'Send the PAM away! A good riddance! That's all. Good-bye!'

And the mer-king said: 'We don't want to lose you, but we think you ought to go.' And Artaxerxes felt very small and unimportant altogether (which was good for him). Even the mer-dog laughed at him.

But funnily enough, Roverandom was quite upset. After all, he had his own reasons for knowing that Artaxerxes' magic was not without effect. And he had bitten the shark's tail, too, hadn't he? And he had started the whole thing with that trouser-bite. And he belonged to the Land himself, and felt it was a bit hard on a poor land-wizard being baited by all these sea-folk.

Anyway he came up to the old fellow and said: 'Please, Mr Artaxerxes – !'

'Well?' said the wizard, quite kindly (he was so glad not to be called PAM, and he had not heard a 'Mister' for weeks). 'Well? What is it, little dog?'

'I beg your pardon, I do really. Awfully sorry, I mean. I never meant to damage your reputation.' Roverandom was thinking of the Sea-serpent and the shark's tail, but (luckily) Artaxerxes thought he was referring to his trousers.

'Come, come!' he said. 'We won't bring up bygones. Least said, soonest mended, or patched. I think we had both better go back home again together.'

'But please, Mr Artaxerxes,' said Roverandom, 'could you bother to turn me back into my proper size?'

'Certainly!' said the wizard, glad to find somebody that still believed he could do anything at all. 'Certainly!

But you are best and safest as you are, while you are down here. Let's get away from this first! And I am really and truly busy just now.'

And he really and truly was. He went into the workshops and collected all his paraphernalia, insignia, symbols, memoranda, books of recipes, arcana, apparatus, and bags and bottles of miscellaneous spells. He burned all that would burn in his waterproof forge; and the rest he tipped into the back-garden. Extraordinary things took place there afterwards: all the flowers went mad, and the vegetables were monstrous, and the fishes that ate them were turned into sea-worms, sea-cats, sea-cows, sea-lions, sea-tigers, sea-devils, porpoises, dugongs, cephalopods, manatees, and calamities, or merely poisoned; and phantasms, visions, bewilderments, illusions, and hallucinations sprouted so thick that nobody had any peace in the palace at all, and they were obliged to move. In fact they began to respect the memory of that wizard after they had lost him. But that was long afterwards. At the moment they were clamouring for him to depart.

When all was ready Artaxerxes said good-bye to the mer-king – rather coldly; and not even the mer-children seemed to mind very much, he had so often been busy, and occasions of the bubbles (like the one I told you about) had been rare. Some of his countless sisters-in-law tried to be polite, especially if Mrs Artaxerxes was there; but really everybody was impatient to see him going out of the gate, so that they could send a humble message to the Sea-serpent:

'The regrettable wizard has departed and will return no more, Your Worship. Pray, go to sleep!'

Of course Mrs Artaxerxes went too. The mer-king had so many daughters that he could afford to lose one without much grief, especially the tenth eldest. He gave her a bag of jewels and a wet kiss on the doorstep and went back to his throne. But everybody else was very sorry, and especially Mrs Artaxerxes' mass of mer-nieces and mer-nephews; and they were also very sorry to lose Roverandom too.

The sorriest of all and the most downcast was the mer-dog: 'Just drop me a line whenever you go to the seaside,' he said, 'and I will pop up and have a look at you.'

'I won't forget!' said Roverandom. And then they went.

The oldest whale was waiting. Roverandom sat on Mrs Artaxerxes' lap, and when they were all settled on the whale's back, off they started.

And all the people said: 'Good-bye!' very loud, and 'A good riddance of bad rubbish' quietly, but not too quietly; and that was the end of Artaxerxes in the office of Pacific and Atlantic Magician. Who has done their bewitchments for them since, I don't know. Old Psamathos and the Man-in-the-Moon, I should think, have managed it between them; they are perfectly capable of it.

5

THE WHALE LANDED on a quiet shore far, far away from the cove of Psamathos; Artaxerxes was most particular about that. There Mrs Artaxerxes and the whale were left, while the wizard (with Roverandom in his pocket) walked a couple of miles or so to the neighbouring seaside town to get an old suit and a green hat and some tobacco, in exchange for the wonderful suit of velvet (which created a sensation in the streets). He also purchased a bath-chair for Mrs Artaxerxes (you must not forget her tail).

'Please, Mr Artaxerxes,' began Roverandom once more, when they were sitting on the beach again in the afternoon. The wizard was smoking a pipe with his back against the whale, looking happier than he had done for a long while, and not at all busy. 'What about my proper shape, if you don't mind? And my proper size, too, please!'

'O very well!' said Artaxerxes. 'I thought I might just have had a nap before getting busy; but I don't mind. Let's get it over! Where's my — ' And then he stopped short. He had suddenly remembered that he had burnt and thrown away all his spells at the bottom of the Deep Blue Sea.

He really was dreadfully upset. He got up and felt in his trouser-pockets, and his waistcoat-pockets, and his coat-pockets, inside and out, and he could not find the least bit of magic anywhere in any of them. (Of course not, the silly old fellow; he was so flustered he had even forgotten that it was only an hour or two since he had bought his suit in a pawnbroker's shop. As a matter of fact it had belonged to, or at any rate had been sold by, an elderly butler, and he had gone through the pockets pretty thoroughly first.)

The wizard sat down and mopped his forehead with a purple handkerchief, looking thoroughly miserable again. 'I really am very, very sorry!' he said. 'I never meant to leave you like this for ever and ever; but now I don't see that it can be helped. Let it be a lesson to you not to bite the trousers of nice kind wizards!'

'Ridiculous nonsense!' said Mrs Artaxerxes. 'Nice kind wizard, indeed! There is no nice or kind or wizard about it, if you don't give the little dog back his shape and size at once – and what's more I shall go back to the bottom of the Deep Blue Sea, and never come back to you again.'

Poor old Artaxerxes looked almost as worried as he did when the Sea-serpent was giving trouble. 'My dear!' he said. 'I'm very sorry, but I went and put my very strongest anti-removal spell-preserver on the dog – after Psamathos began to interfere (drat him!) and just to show him that he can't do everything, and that I won't have sand-rabbit wizards interfering in my private bit of fun – and I quite forgot to save the antidote when I was clearing up down below! I used to keep it in a little black bag hanging on the door in my workshop.

'Dear, dear me! I am sure you'll agree that it was only meant to be a bit of fun,' he said, turning to Roverandom, and his old nose got very large and red with his distress.

He went on saying 'dear, dear, deary me!' and shaking his head and beard; and he never noticed that Roverandom was not taking any notice, and the whale was winking. Mrs Artaxerxes had got up and gone to her luggage, and now she was laughing and holding out an old black bag in her hand.

'Now stop waggling your beard, and get to business!' she said. But when Artaxerxes saw the bag, he was too surprised for a moment to do anything but look at it with his old mouth wide open.

'Come along!' said his wife. 'It is your bag, isn't it? I picked it up, and several other little oddments that belonged to *me*, on the nasty rubbish heap you made in the garden.' She opened the bag to peep inside, and out jumped the wizard's magic fountain-pen wand, and also a cloud of funny smoke came out, twisting itself into strange shapes and curious faces.

Then Artaxerxes woke up. 'Here, give it to me! You're wasting it!' he cried; and he grabbed Roverandom by the scruff of his neck, and popped him kicking and yapping into the bag, before you could say 'knife'. Then he turned the bag round three times, waving the pen in the other hand, and —

'Thank you! That'll do nicely!' he said, and opened the bag.

There was a loud bang, and lo! and behold! there was no bag, only Rover, just as he had always been before he first met the wizard that morning on the lawn. Well, perhaps not just the same; he was a bit bigger, as he was now some months older.

It is no good trying to describe how excited he felt, or how funny and smaller everything seemed, even the oldest whale; nor how strong and ferocious Rover felt. For just one moment he looked longingly at the wizard's trousers; but he did not want the story to begin all over again, so, after he had run a mile in circles for joy, and nearly barked his head off, he came back and said 'Thank you!'; and he even added 'Very pleased to have met you', which was very polite indeed.

'That's all right!' said Artaxerxes. 'And that's the last magic I shall do. I'm going to retire. And *you* had better be getting home. I have no magic left to send you home with, so you'll have to walk. But that won't hurt a strong young dog.'

So Rover said good-bye, and the whale winked, and Mrs Artaxerxes gave him a piece of cake; and that was the last he saw of them for a long while. Long, long afterwards, when he was visiting a seaside place that he had never been to before, he found out what had happened to them; for they were there. Not the whale, of course, but the retired wizard and his wife.

They had settled in that seaside town, and Artaxerxes, taking the name of Mr A. Pam, had set up a cigarette and chocolate shop near the beach – but he was very, very careful never to touch the water (even fresh water, and that he found no hardship). A poor trade for a wizard, but he did at least try to clear up the nasty mess that his customers made on the beach; and he made a good deal of money out of 'Pam's Rock', which was very pink and sticky. There may have been the least bit of magic in it, for children liked it so much they went on eating it even after they had dropped it in the sand.

But Mrs Artaxerxes, I should say Mrs A. Pam, made much more money. She kept bathing-tents and vans, and gave swimming lessons, and drove home in a bath-chair drawn by white ponies, and wore the mer-king's jewels in the afternoon, and became very famous, so that no one ever alluded to her tail.

In the meanwhile, however, Rover is plodding down the country lanes and highways, going along following his nose, which is bound to lead him home in the end, as dogs' noses do.

'All the Man-in-the-Moon's dreams don't come true, then – just as he said himself,' thought Rover as he padded along. 'This was evidently one that didn't. I don't even know the name of the place where the little boys live, and that's a pity.'

The dry land, he found, was often as dangerous a place for a dog as the moon or the ocean, though much duller. Motor after motor racketed by, filled (Rover thought) with the same people, all making all speed (and all dust and all smell) to somewhere.

'I don't believe half of them know where they are going to, or why they are going there, or would know it if they got there,' grumbled Rover as he coughed and choked; and his feet got tired on the hard, gloomy, black roads. So he turned into the fields, and had many mild adventures of the bird and rabbit sort in an aimless kind of way, and more than one enjoyable fight with other dogs, and several hurried flights from larger dogs.

And so at last, weeks or months since the tale began (he could not have told you which), he got back to his own garden gate. And there was the little boy playing on the lawn with the yellow ball! And the dream had come true, just as he had never expected!!

'There's Roverandom!!!' cried little boy Two with a shout.

And Rover sat up and begged, and could not find his voice to bark anything, and the little boy kissed his head, and went dashing into the house, crying: 'Here's my little begging dog come back large and real!!!'

He told his grandmother all about it. How was Rover to know that he had belonged to the little boys' grandmother all the while? He had only belonged to her a month or two, when he was bewitched. But I wonder how much Psamathos and Artaxerxes had known about it?

The grandmother (very surprised indeed as she was at her dog's return looking so well and not motor-smashed or lorry-flattened at all) did not understand what on earth the little boy was talking about; though he told her all he knew about it very exactly, and over and over again. She gathered with a great deal of trouble (she was of course just the wee-est bit deaf) that the dog was to be called Roverandom and not Rover, because the Man-in-the-Moon said so ('What odd ideas the child has, to be sure'); and that he belonged not to her after all but to little boy Two, because mummy brought him home with the shrimps ('Very well, my dear, if you like; but I thought I bought him from the gardener's brother's son').

I haven't told you all their argument, of course; it was long and complicated, as it often is when both sides are right. All that you want to know is that he *was* called Roverandom after that, and he *did* belong to the little boy, and went back, when the boys' visit to their grandmother was over, to the house where he had once sat on the chest-of-drawers. He never did *that* again, of course. He lived sometimes in the country and sometimes, most of the time, in the white house on the cliff by the sea.

He got to know old Psamathos very well, never well enough to leave out the P, but well enough, when he was grown up to a large and dignified dog, to dig him up out of the sand and his sleep and have many and many a chat with him. Indeed Roverandom grew to be very wise, and had an immense local reputation, and had all sorts of other adventures (many of which the little boy shared).

But the ones I have told you about were probably the most unusual and the most exciting. Only Tinker says she does not believe a word of them. Jealous cat!

THE END

Notes

In the introduction and notes, page references
are to the first edition of the work cited.

xi **newspaper reports.** The *Times* of 7 September 1925 reported that 'at Whitley Bay all the amusement stalls and boat landings were smashed and the beach was strewn with wood and iron. . . . The sea waves rose to a height of 40 feet at Hornsea, tearing away seats from alcoves on the new promenade and flooding fields over a large area. The South Beach bathing pool at Scarborough had big coping stones knocked off' – and so forth. The forecast had been for occasional showers.

the five illustrations he made for the story. The original art is in the Bodleian Library, Oxford University, as MS Tolkien Drawings 88, fol. 25 (*Lunar Landscape*); 89, fol. 1 (untitled, 'Rover Arrives on the Moon'); 89, fol. 2 (*House Where 'Rover' Began His Adventures as a 'Toy'*); 89, fol. 3 (*The White Dragon Pursues Roverandom & the Moondog*); and 89, fol. 4 (*The Gardens of the Merking's Palace*).

xii **'Father Christmas' letters.** The majority of these were published in 1976 as *The Father Christmas Letters*, edited by Baillie Tolkien.

snapdragon. In this sense 'a game or amusement (usually held at Christmas) consisting of snatching raisins out of a bowl or dish of burning brandy or other spirit and eating them whilst alight' (*Oxford English Dictionary*).

xv **almost certainly the text . . . report dated 7 January 1937.** Rayner Unwin's report cites the name 'Psamathos' and the price '6d' (sixpence), features which did not enter the text of *Roverandom* until the second (fragmentary) and third (complete) typescripts.

There were also the stories. See further, *J.R.R. Tolkien: A Biography* by Humphrey Carpenter (1977), pp. 161 ff.

3 **bone-and-bottle men.** Itinerant collectors of bones and bottles, or of other materials (cf. *rag-and-bone man*) which they sold for a living, e.g. to paper and bone mills.

the blue feather stuck in the back of the green hat. Tom Bombadil, the hero of an early story by Tolkien and a character in *The Lord of the Rings* (1954–5), also wears a hat with a blue feather.

5 **Only after midnight could he walk.** The fantasy that toys come to life at night, or when no one is looking, appears in many stories, such as 'The Steadfast Tin Soldier' by Hans Christian Andersen (1838) and 'The Wax Doll' by E.H. Knatchbull-Hugessen (1869).

Mark him sixpence. In the first typescript, Rover was marked 'fourpence'. This was altered to 'sixpence' in the second typescript, perhaps a reflection of increased prices during the years we suppose to have elapsed between these drafts.

tea-time. Around 4:00 p.m.; when a light afternoon meal of tea, bread, cakes, etc. is served. Cf. 'tea-timish', p. 15.

6 **She had three boys.** The mother of course is Edith (Mrs. J.R.R.) Tolkien, and her three boys are John, Michael, and Christopher. Michael is the one 'particularly fond of little dogs'.

screwed up in paper. Wrapped for the customer in paper screwed up tight at the ends.

7 **the best dog-language he could manage.** The eponymous fairies of Lewis Carroll's *Sylvie and Bruno* stories (1889–93), which Tolkien enjoyed, speak fluent 'doggee'.

8 **Rover was put on a chair by the bedside.** In the earliest extant draft of this part (the first typescript) Rover is put instead on a *chest-of-drawers*. Tolkien may have felt that this was too great a height from which Rover would have to jump down, even onto a bed, to explore the house – and which he would have had to scale before morning. Rover was, after all, a toy dog, and very small (although he seems sometimes to be larger). The phrase on p. 9, 'he [the boy] saw Rover sitting on the chest-of-drawers', is a survival of the earlier draft, to which Tolkien added a slightly awkward explanation 'where he had put him while he was dressing'. Tolkien let stand the reference on p. 89 to 'the house where he had once sat on the chest-of-drawers'.

the moon rose up out of the sea, and laid the silver path across the waters that is the way to places at the edge of the world and beyond, for those that can walk on it. This invention may have been Tolkien's own, but it bears a striking resemblance to the 'bright moon-path stretching from the dark earth . . . toward the moon' that appears in *The Garden behind the Moon* by the American writer and artist Howard Pyle (1895). The principal character in that book walks from the shore along the path of light and visits the Man-in-the-Moon. In *Roverandom* Rover does not himself walk on the moon-path, but is carried above it. – See also above, pp. ix, x.

9 **little boy Two.** Michael, the Tolkiens' second son.

11 ***Psamathists.*** In the earliest (manuscript) text the sand-sorcerer is called a *Psammead*, a word borrowed directly from the 'sand-fairy' of E. Nesbit's *Five Children and It* (1902) and *The Story of the Amulet* (1906). Like Tolkien's psamathist, Nesbit's psammead has a gruff but whimsical personality and likes nothing better than to sleep in the warm sand. In the first typescript Tolkien sometimes spelled *psammead* as *samyad*, and very briefly called Psamathos a *nilbog* (*goblin* spelled backwards). In the second typescript Psamathos is called by name or is only 'the psamathist'.

Psamathos Psamathides. *Psamathos*, *Psamathides*, and *Psamathist* each contain the Greek root *psammos* 'sand'. *Psamathos* comes, appropriately for the habits of this creature, from the Greek for 'sea-sand'. *Psamathides* contains the patronymic *-ides* 'son of', and *Psamathist* the suffix *-ist* 'one who devotes himself to a branch of knowledge' (as in *philologist*); hence, roughly, *Psamathos Psamathides* 'Sandy, the son of Sandy', *Psamathist* 'expert on sand'.

not more than the tip of one of his long ears stuck out. The psamathist's 'long ears' were 'horns' in all versions, until altered on the final typescript. Nesbit's psammead has eyes 'on long horns like a snail's eyes'.

13 **'I am Psamathos Psamathides, the chief of all the Psamathists!' He said this several times very proudly, pronouncing every letter, and with every *P* he blew a cloud of sand down his nose.** Cf. p. 11, 'a great fuss he made about the proper pronunciation'.

Tolkien is making a joke of the fact that in *Psamathos*, *Psamathides*, and *Psamathists*, 'correctly' pronounced, the *P* of *Ps* is silent. The *Oxford English Dictionary* argues that dropping the *p* in *ps* words in English is 'an unscholarly practice often leading to ambiguity or to a disguising of the composition of the word', and therefore recommends the *p* in optional pronunciations for all Greek loan-words except the *psalm*, *psalter* group.

14 **Artaxerxes.** An appropriate name, given the wizard's country of origin (see the following note), shared by three kings of Persia in the fifth and fourth centuries B.C. and the founder of the Sassanid dynasty in the third century B.C.

He comes from Persia . . . put him on the way to Pershore instead. . . . They say he is a nimble plum-gatherer. Pershore is a small town near Evesham in Worcestershire. Tolkien is playing, of course, on the near-homonyms *Persia* and *Pershore*; but also it is significant that the Vale of Evesham is noted for its plums (including the yellow Pershore variety), and that Tolkien's brother Hilary owned an orchard and market garden near Evesham and for many years tended plum-trees. – 'Nimble plum-gatherer' suggests that Artaxerxes was good at getting hold of the best or choicest things.

cider. In England, an alcoholic drink made from the fermented juice of apples. Some say that the best cider comes from the west of England, including the Vale of Evesham.

15 **marrows.** Vegetable marrows, in America often called *gourds* or *summer squash*.

17 **Mew.** Another word for *gull*.

18 **very tall black cliffs of sheer rock.** Near Filey are Speeton and Bempton, both noted for their lofty cliffs (400 ft. sheer drop), breeding places of innumerable sea-birds; but these are chalk cliffs, not black. Uninhabited islands with similar cliffs and bird colonies are common along the coasts of northern Britain.

20 **the Isle of Dogs.** The real Isle of Dogs is a tongue of land which projects into the River Thames in south-east London. Its name, on which Tolkien is playing, may have come from Henry VIII or Elizabeth I having kept hounds there when in residence across the river at Greenwich.

21 **There is at least one dog, for the Man-in-the-Moon keeps one.** This agrees with some traditions; cf. Shakespeare, *A Midsummer Night's Dream* v, i: 'This man, with lantern, dog, and bush of thorn, / Presenteth Moonshine'.

22 **Rover could see a white tower . . . an old man with a long silvery beard.** In 'The Tale of the Sun and Moon' in *The Book of Lost Tales* Tolkien wrote of the vessel of the moon which sails through the sky, and in which 'an aged Elf with hoary locks' stowed away; 'and there dwells he ever since . . . , and a little white turret has he builded on the Moon where often he climbs and watches the heavens, or the world beneath. . . . Some indeed have named him the Man in the Moon . . .' (*Part One* [1983], pp. 192–3). In Tolkien's poem 'Why the Man in the Moon Came Down Too Soon' (published 1923) the Man lives in a 'pallid minaret / Dizzy and white at its lunar height / In a world of silver set'; see *The Book of Lost Tales, Part One*, pp. 204–6. An illustration of this scene, with the Man sliding earthward along a 'spidery hair' (cf. the 'silver threads and ropes' woven by moon-spiders, *Roverandom* p. 25), is reproduced in *J.R.R. Tolkien: Artist & Illustrator* by Wayne G. Hammond and Christina Scull (1995), p. 49.

24 **called Rover after me.** Tolkien is playing on two different meanings of this phrase. The moon-dog's 'So you are called Rover after me?' is taken by Roverandom to mean 'So you are called Rover in my honour'. But in the rejoinder 'so you must have been called Rover after me' the moon-dog means 'chronologically later'.

25 **the moon was just passing under the world.** On this point, see p. xix above, and *The Book of Lost Tales, Part One*, p. 216 ('the Moon dares not the utter loneliness of the outer dark . . . and he journeys still beneath the world').

Don't worry the moonbeams, and don't kill my white rabbits. And come home when you feel hungry. Such a prohibition combined with advice is one characteristic of the traditional fairy-tale. The Man-in-the-Moon's warning is repeated in various forms, and later is echoed in Mrs Artaxerxes' words: 'Don't worry the fire-fish', etc. (p. 63).

27 **It was a long time before he found out.** In fact we never learn why Psamathos sent Rover to the moon. The earliest text has: 'He never found it all out, for wizards often have deep reasons that are

not found out by generations of cats, let alone of dogs – and what he did find took a long while.'

sword-flies, and glass-beetles. One is reminded of the Rocking-horse-fly, Snap-dragon-fly, and Bread-and-butter-fly in Lewis Carroll's *Through the Looking Glass* (1872). Cf. also *flutterbies* (a reversal of *butterflies*, but akin to *flittermice* or bats), p. 28, and *diamond-beetles* and *ruby-moths*, p. 40.

fifty-seven varieties. An allusion to the Heinz Co.'s famous fifty-seven varieties of packaged foods.

28 **a faint thin music.** Music contributes greatly to the atmosphere of *Roverandom*: it is made by the flora on the white side of the moon, the nightingales and children in the garden on the dark side (p. 41), and the mer-folk under the sea (p. 59). The (real and fanciful) floral names in this paragraph suggest music or musical instruments: bells, whistles, trumpets, horns, fiddles, brass, reeds (woodwinds). *Ringaroses* recalls the nursery rhyme 'Ring-a-ring o'roses'. 'Rhymeroyals and pennywhistles' echoes *pennyroyal*, the creeping mint *Mentha pulegium*, as well as *rhyme royal*, in poetry a seven-line iambic pentameter stanza. *Polyphonies* is a play on *polypodies* (ferns of the genus *Polypodium*) as well as on *polyphony*, a term for contrapuntal music. *Brasstongues* suggests the fern *hart's-tongue* and also recalls 1 Corinthians 13:1, 'Though I speak with the tongues of men and of angels, and have not charity, I am become as sounding brass or a tinkling cymbal'. *Cracken* is a variation (implying a sound) on *bracken*.

they were roofed with pale blue leaves that never fell. . . . Later in the year the trees all burst together into pale golden blossoms. . . . A foreshadowing, perhaps, of the mallorn trees of Lothlórien in *The Lord of the Rings* (bk. 2, ch. 6): 'For in the autumn their leaves fall not, but turn to gold.'

29 **an enormous white elephant.** Possibly a reference to the case of Sir Paul Neale, a seventeenth-century virtuoso who claimed to have discovered an elephant in the moon, only to find that a mouse, which he mistook for an elephant, had crept inside his telescope.

31 **the chimneys there . . . and the black smoke; and the red furnace fires!** Both Birmingham in Tolkien's youth, and Leeds in which he and his family lived when *Roverandom* was conceived, were dirty, smoky, industrial cities, now much cleaner.

32 **rat and rabbit it.** A vulgar imprecation, appropriate for a dog with 'low tastes' (p. 31). *Rat* is from *od rat* 'God rot' = *drat*; *rabbit* is an alteration of *rat* with the same meaning.

they took the first shelter they came to, and no precautions. Cf. *The Hobbit*, ch. 4, in which the company take shelter in a cave without thoroughly exploring it: 'That, of course, is the dangerous part about caves: you don't know how far they go back, sometimes, or where a passage behind may lead to, or what is waiting for you inside.'

33 **He [the White Dragon] fought the Red Dragon in Caerdragon in Merlin's time . . . after which the other dragon was Very Red.** Legend tells how the British King Vortigern tried to build a tower near Mount Snowdon for defense against his enemies, but what was built each day fell down each night. The young Merlin advised Vortigern to uncover a pool at the tower's foundations, and then to have the pool drained. At the bottom of the pool were two sleeping dragons, one white, the other red, who upon awakening engaged in combat. The red dragon, said Merlin, was the British people, and the white dragon the Saxons, who would prevail. The red dragon would then be 'very red' – that is, bloody in defeat. This was supposed to take place at Dinas Emrys, in Gwynedd, Wales, here called *Caerdragon*, 'castle [or fortress] of the dragon'. The manuscript has *Caervyrddin* 'Myrddin's [Merlin's] fort' (i.e. Carmarthen, Dyfed), altered in writing to ?*Caerddreichion*; this was crossed through, and changed to the equivalent *Caerdragon* in the first typescript.

the Three Islands. From Welsh *Teir Ynys Prydein*, in which *ynys* (literally 'island') means 'realm', hence the Three Realms of Britain: England, Scotland, and Wales.

Snowdon. The highest peak in Wales (3560 ft.), located in Snowdonia National Park, Gwynedd. Tolkien's remark about a man who left a bottle on top of Snowdon is a reference to the mountain's attractiveness to tourists, and so to their litter. In the first text Tolkien wrote of visitors to Snowdon 'smoking cigarettes and drinking ginger beer and leaving the bottles about'.

Gwynfa, some time after King Arthur's disappearance, at a time when dragons' tails were esteemed a great delicacy by the Saxon Kings. Welsh *gwynfa* (or *gwynva*) is literally 'white (or blessed) place', poetically 'paradise' or 'heaven'. We have been unable to find a Gwynfa in legend or folklore to suit its use in *Roverandom*; but its conjunction here with 'King Arthur's disappearance' (the earliest text reads 'King Arthur's death'), i.e. his removal to an otherworld (Avalon), suggests that Gwynfa is a place of this kind, 'not so far from the world's edge'. Perhaps cf. Gwynvyd, the heavenly upperworld in Welsh tradition. Or it may be simply that a 'white place' is where a white dragon would go, and that its name is a play on *Snowdon*, literally 'snow hill'. – The notion of dragon's tail as a delicacy occurs also (and in draft, more or less contemporaneously) in *Farmer Giles of Ham*: 'It was still the custom for Dragon's Tail to be served up at the King's Christmas Feast' (published 1949, p. 22). But that story takes place before the days of the Saxon kings. – Tolkien seems to imply that the dragon went away to avoid being hunted for his tail. But 'when dragons' tails were esteemed' etc. also served to introduce in the first typescript a (deleted) comment on 'Saxon Kings': 'a fierce race [i.e. the Saxons] that some Frenchmen don't believe ever existed'. Christopher Tolkien suggested to us that this phrase may be a criticism of the French scholar Emile Legouis; and indeed, in the history of English literature by Legouis and his colleague Louis Cazamian published in England in 1926 (earlier in French) is an argument that the Anglo-Saxons were a quiet, settled people (i.e. not a 'fierce race'), and that it is illusory to find in their literature a 'reflection of Germanic barbarism'.

34 **turn the whole moon red.** When in eclipse the moon sometimes takes on a copper-red hue.

The mountains rocked . . . waterfalls stood still. After this in the final text, but marked for deletion, is: 'no young man's motor-bicycle going through a sleeping suburb could have done more'.

like the sails that ships had when they still were ships and not steam-engines. The dragon in *The Faerie Queene* by Edmund Spenser (1590) has wings 'like two sayles, in which the hollow wynd / Is gathered full, and worketh speedy way: / And eke the pennes, that did his pineons bynd, / Were like mayne-yardes with flying canvas lynd'.

flapping like a flapdragon and snapping like a snapdragon. In this sense both *flapdragon* and *snapdragon* refer to a representation of a dragon or dragon's head constructed to open and shut its mouth, and carried by mummers at Christmas or in mayoral or civic shows and processions.

35 **Fifth of November.** When Britain celebrates, with fireworks and bonfires, the discovery and prevention in 1605 of a Catholic plot to blow up Parliament. It is also called 'Guy Fawkes Night' after the best-known of the conspirators.

36 **The next eclipse was a failure.** On this point, see p. xiii. – It remains a mystery how the Man-in-the-Moon coordinates the Great White Dragon's eclipse-making so that it conforms to a schedule ('They will bring on an eclipse before it is due!' and 'the dragon was too busy licking his tummy to attend to it', pp. 35, 36). But long before *Roverandom* there was a tradition in various mythologies that eclipses were caused by dragons – devouring, not just obscuring, the moon or sun.

40 **real colour.** In 'Why the Man in the Moon Came Down Too Soon' (see p. 94, note for p. 22) the Man is 'tired . . . of his pallid minaret . . . He had wearily longed for fire: / Not the limpid lights of wan selenites / But a red terrestrial pyre / with impurpurate glows of crimson and rose / And leaping orange tongue; / For great seas of blues and the passionate hues / When a dancing dawn is young.'

owls like eagles. There is in fact an 'eagle-owl', a large, fierce species which occasionally visits Britain from Scandinavia. Its upper parts are blackish brown.

bob-owlers. Thick-bodied moths (West Midlands dialect).

42 **a garden in twilight.** On the similarity of the moon-garden to the Cottage of Lost Play in *The Book of Lost Tales*, see p. xviii. – In Howard Pyle's *The Garden behind the Moon* the hero, David, also visits the Man-in-the-Moon's back-garden, where children romp and play and shout. Here, as in *Roverandom*, the children seem to have travelled to the garden while asleep, for their real bodies remain on earth. David reaches the garden however in a more prosaic way than Roverandom: by the back stairs in the Man-in-the-Moon's house.

the children don't come by your way . . . but not in this valley. On the 'Path of Dreams', see p. xviii. – The earliest text included, in rough working: '"This is the valley of happy dreamers," said the

Man. "There is another one but we are not going to look at that, and most people who see it forget it luckily. Some of the dreams they have here last for ever. . . ."' > 'I make most of the dreams. Some they bring with 'em, and some, I regret to say, the spiders make – but not in this valley, and not if I catch 'em at it. This is the valley of Happy Dreams.'

45 **Mother Hubbard's dead dog.** The nursery rhyme *Old Mother Hubbard* includes the lines 'But when she came back / The poor dog was dead. . . . She went to the tavern / For white wine and red; / But when she came back / The dog stood on his head.'

46 **At last they came to the grey edge.** In *Roverandom* the moon has distinct 'white' and 'dark' sides, and apparently these stay this way all the time: one side 'dark with a pale sky', the other 'pale with a dark sky'. The real moon of course experiences night and day (if at a different rate than the Earth), and the 'dark side' is 'dark' not because it receives no light, but because it always faces away from the Earth, and so was unseen until the days of lunar orbiters. Although the Earth of the story is flat (see p. xix), the moon is clearly a sphere: Roverandom falls straight through it to the dark side, and as he and the Man-in-the-Moon walk home they see an earthrise. – John Tolkien does not recall that either he or his brother Michael was bothered by anomalies when the tale was told to them, and points out that *Roverandom* was of course written for young children, to whom such matters are merely part of the wonder of the story.

49 **News of the World.** A British newspaper known for its sensationalism.

51 **He fell in love with the rich mer-king's elderly but lovely daughter.** A play on the lyric 'So I fell in love with a rich attorney's elderly ugly daughter', from the Gilbert and Sullivan opera *Trial by Jury* (1871).

Proteus, Poseidon, Triton, Neptune. Proteus and Poseidon were gods of the sea in Greek mythology. Neptune is the equivalent of Poseidon in Roman mythology. Triton was also a sea-god, the son of Poseidon, but also a merman in Greek tradition.

Niord. A Norse sea-deity. 'His silly marriage' is a reference to a story told in the *Gylfaginning* and *Skáldskarpmál* of the *Younger Edda* by Snorri Sturluson (1178/9–1241). The gods promised a giant's daughter that she could marry one of them as compensation for the killing of her father by Thor, but she was allowed to see only the feet of her prospective bridegroom before making her choice. She chose the most beautiful feet, hoping to get Balder, the most beautiful of the gods, but the feet were Niord's. There seems to have been some speculation among commentators as to why Niord had better feet than Balder; Tolkien's comment that the giantess chose Niord because he had clean feet '(so convenient in the home)' is a joke, of course, but Tolkien's colleague at Leeds, E.V. Gordon, in a note in his *Introduction to Old Norse* (1927, in which Tolkien is thanked for his advice), remarked that Niord had the cleanest feet because he was god of the sea (presumably Gordon meant that they were regularly washed).

the Old Man of the Sea. A character in the *Arabian Nights*, found by Sindbad the Sailor when he was shipwrecked on his fifth voyage. The Old Man asks to be carried across a river, but when Sindbad complies he finds it impossible to get the Man off his back. Sindbad frees himself by getting the Man drunk and then killing him with a rock.

a floating mine . . . a year or two ago, right on one of the buttons! A mine of the sort placed in waters during the First World War. (Evidently the Old Man of the Sea tried to be 'carried' on one.) Its 'buttons' are spike-like detonators.

51 **Humpty Dumpty.** The egg in the nursery rhyme, whom 'All the king's horses / And all the king's men' couldn't put together again after he is broken.

52 **I thought Britannia ruled the waves. . . . She prefers patting lions on the beach, and sitting on a penny with an eel-fork in her hand.** Britannia, who 'rules the waves' in popular song, is a symbol of Great Britain, usually depicted as a seated woman with a shield, a trident (the 'eel-fork'), and a lion. She has appeared on British coins and medals since the reign of Charles II.

don't . . . forget your Ps. Literally, do not forget to pronounce the first letter of 'Psamathos'. But since this story began with Rover failing to say 'please' to Artaxerxes, and the phrase 'to mind your Ps and Qs' means to be on good behaviour, the Man-in-the-Moon is also making a joke.

they were at least coloured. Newspapers at this time were not printed in colour. – *The Illustrated Weekly Weed*, in the list of mer-folk newspapers, suggests *The Illustrated London News*.

57 **pot and jam him.** 'To pot' is slang for 'to shoot or kill for the pot'; 'to jam' is slang for 'to hang'.

58 **Uin the oldest of the Right Whales.** See p. xix. In whalers' jargon a *right whale* is the right kind to kill, i.e. of the family *Balaenidae*, rich in whalebone and easily captured.

61 **PAM.** A reference to the nickname of the renowned British politician and Prime Minister, Lord Palmerston (1784–1865).

62 **sea-dog.** Here literally a dog, of course, but Tolkien is alluding to the word as slang, 'sailor'.

64 **limpets.** Marine gastropods which cling tightly to rocks, but also 'officials alleged to be superfluous but clinging to their offices' (*Oxford English Dictionary*).

a minor art but still needing a deal of practice. Tolkien is suggesting that Artaxerxes' magic has its limitations. In the earliest text the passage preceding these words includes a clarifying extra phrase, here italicized: 'Artaxerxes was a really good magician in his own way, *the conjuring-trick sort* (or Rover would never have had these adventures).' In his essay *On Fairy-Stories* (first published 1947) Tolkien wrote with disdain of 'high class conjuring', as opposed to true magic (of which Psamathos and the Man-in-the-Moon were capable).

65 **it was a long ship . . . and he called it the Red Worm.** The mer-dog's story derives in part from the thirteenth-century saga of Olaf Tryggvason in the *Heimskringla* by Snorri Sturluson. In that work Olaf Tryggvason, King of Norway 995–1000 A.D., is defeated in a sea battle. He leaps from his famous ship, the Long Serpent (or Long Worm), but legend says that he did not drown, but swam to safety and eventually died as a monk in Greece or Syria. In the manuscript of *Roverandom* the ship is in fact called 'Long Worm', and Tolkien mentioned King Olaf's ship by this name in the lecture on dragons he gave in January 1938 at the University Museum, Oxford. – King Olaf had a famous dog, Vige, who died of grief when his master disappeared.

66 **the mermaids caught him.** According to legend, mermaids are eager to drag mortals under the sea, where they keep their souls captive. Tolkien distinguishes 'golden-haired mermaids' from 'dark-haired sirens' (p. 61), their mythological precursors.

67 **the Orkneys.** A group of islands to the north-east of Scotland, settled by the Vikings in the eighth and ninth centuries and brought under the Scottish crown in 1476.

70 **This is the Pacific, I believe.** Indeed, all of the places the mer-dog names are in or on the Pacific Ocean: Japan; Honolulu, Hawaii; Manila, The Philippines; Easter Island, west of Peru; Thursday Island, off the northern tip of Queensland, Australia; and Vladivostok, Russia.

explosions occur in the sea-bed. An undersea eruption occurred on Santorini (Thera) in the Aegean Sea in August 1925, the month before *Roverandom* was first told.

71 **the wizard would have changed him into a sea-slug, or sent him to the Back of Beyond . . . or even to Pot.** In the earliest text it is said that Roverandom 'didn't know that while Araxerxes' strongest spell was on him the wizard could do no more bewitching of him'; but this made no sense, as Artaxerxes had already 'bewitched' Roverandom a second time, when he changed him into a sea-dog. – The 'Back of Beyond' is any place ever so far off, very out of the way. 'To go to pot' is to be ruined or destroyed, but since later in the story we are told that Pot is one of only two caves big enough to contain the great Sea-Serpent, Tolkien perhaps also thought of northern dialect *pot* 'deep hole, abyss, pit of hell'.

73 **the Shadowy Seas . . . and the light of Faery upon the waves.** See pp. xviii–xix. The earliest text has: 'It was the whale who took them to the Bay of Fairyland beyond the Magic Isles, and they saw far off in the West the Shores of Fairyland, and the Mountains of the Last Land and the light of fairyland upon the waves.' In Tolkien's mythology the Shadowy Seas and the Magic Isles hide and guard Aman (Elvenhome, and the home of the Valar or Gods) from the rest of the world. A good illustration of this geography, from the 1930s, is in Tolkien's *Ambarkanta* (*The Shaping of Middle-earth*, 1986, p. 249).

74 **Outer Lands**. See p. xix. In earlier drafts Tolkien used the phrase 'ordinary lands'.

The only thing he did like a fish was to drink. That is, he drank alcohol excessively.

75 **the ancient Sea-serpent was waking . . . some people say he would reach from Edge to Edge**. A reference to the Midgard serpent of Norse mythology, which winds itself around the world, but cf. Leviathan in *Job* 41 ('When he raiseth up himself, the mighty are afraid'). – Tolkien could not make up his mind whether or not to capitalize *edge* when referring to one end of the flat world of *Roverandom*. We have regularized all instances as *edge* except 'Edge to Edge' on p. 75, where the capital letters are meant to clarify the meaning of the phrase.

76 **autothalassic**. Sprung from the sea. The list from *primordial* to *silly* is a summary of scholars' conclusions about sea-serpents,and reminiscent of a comment Tolkien made in his 1936 lecture *The Monsters and the Critics* about the 'conflicting babel' of critical opinions about *Beowulf*.

at least one continent fell into the sea. Presumably Atlantis, as the drowned island of Númenor had not yet entered Tolkien's mythology in 1927, and the quoted phrase is already present in the earliest text of *Roverandom*.

he saw the tip of the Sea-serpent's tail sticking out of the entrance . . . That was quite enough for him. Cf. *Farmer Giles of Ham*: '[Garm] ran indeed slap into the tail of [the dragon] Chrysophylax Dives, who had just landed. Never did a dog turn his own tail round and bolt home swifter than Garm' (pp. 25–6).

before the Worm turned again. A play on the proverb 'even a worm will turn' (even the weakest creature will turn upon its tormentors if driven to it), here applied literally to the powerful Sea-serpent. In Anglo-Saxon and Norse myth *worm* (*wyrm*) was a common word for a dragon or serpent.

77 **periwinkles**. Gastropod molluscs, of the genus *littorina*, with shells shaped like spinning tops.

by the skin of their feet. A reference to the dogs' webbed feet, playing on the proverbial 'skin of their teeth'.

78 **trying absentmindedly to get the tip of his tail in his mouth.** Here Tolkien recalls the *ouroboros*, an ancient symbol of unity, renewal, eternity in the form of a serpent devouring its own tail.

81 **sea-worms, sea-cats, sea-cows . . . and calamities.** Tolkien seems to be suggesting that fishes have been turned by Artaxerxes' magic into creatures not entirely of the sea (as Artaxerxes himself is not). In fact most of these, despite their names, are actual marine fauna.

83 **bath-chair.** A large chair on wheels, for use by invalids.

What about my proper shape. The thirteen paragraphs following Roverandom's request were largely an addition in the second version (first typescript). In the earliest the wizard simply 'picked Roverandom up and turned him round three times and said "Thank you, that'll do nicely" — and Roverandom found he was back just as he always was before he first met Artaxerxes that morning on the lawn.' But this would have portrayed Artaxerxes (having also in this version destroyed his spells) as rather better than a 'conjurer'; see p. 102, note for p. 64.

86 **Pam's rock.** Rock (American *rock candy*), a hard candied sugar traditionally sold in stick form at British seaside resorts. The more usual sort is white inside with a thin, sticky pink outer layer, and often the name of the seaside (perhaps in this case the name PAM) running through the white core in a contrasting candy.

87 **bathing tents and vans.** In the 1920s, for modesty's sake, no one changed into swimming clothes on the beach. Some changed in tents, others in vans drawn up to the water's edge. The bather entered the van through a door facing the shore, changed inside, and then left through another door into the sea.

Motor after motor . . . all making all speed (and all dust and all smell) to somewhere. *Motor* 'motorcar'. – Throughout *Roverandom* Tolkien shows his concern about pollution and the effects of industrialization. The man on top of Snowdon was a litterbug; fuel oil gave Niord a dreadful cough; Artaxerxes is commended for cleaning up the mess his customers leave on the beach; and here the traffic, although much less at the time of *Roverandom* than it is today, was still too much for Tolkien's liking. Cf. his poem *Progress in Bimble Town* (published 1931), which according to Carpenter (*Biography*, pp. 105–6) reflects Tolkien's feelings towards Filey after a visit there in 1922. In Bimble Town he saw in the shop windows

> cigarettes, and gum one chews
> (wrapped in paper, cased in card,
> for folk to strew on grass and shore);
> loud garages, where toiling hard
> grimy people bang and roar,
> and engines buzz, and the lights flare,
> all night long – a merry noise!
>   Sometimes through it (this is rare)
> one can hear the shouts of boys;
> sometimes late, when motor-bikes
> are not passing with a screech,
> one hears faintly (if one likes)
> the sea still at it on the beach.
> At what? At churning orange-rind,
> piling up banana-skins,
> gnawing paper, trying to grind
> a broth of bottles, packets, tins,
> before a new day comes with more,
> before next morning's charabangs,
> stopping at the old inn-door
> with reek and rumble, hoots and clangs,
> bring more folk to Godknowswhere
> and Theydontcare, to Bimble Town
> where the steep street, that once was fair,
> with many houses staggers down.